Richards Free Library

Paul Pillsbury
Memorial Book Fund

August 8, 1997

THE TRESPASSERS

Also by Zilpha Keatley Snyder

The
TRESPASSERS

Zilpha Keatley Snyder

DELACORTE PRESS

With thanks to the helpful people at the public library
and middle school in Carmel, California,
who gave me so much good advice.

Published by
Delacorte Press
Bantam Doubleday Dell Publishing Group, Inc.
1540 Broadway
New York, New York 10036

LIBRARY OF CONGRESS CATALOGING-IN-PUBLICATION DATA

Snyder, Zilpha Keatley.
The trespassers / by Zilpha Keatley Snyder.
p.   cm.
Summary: Having trespassed and explored the empty Hutchinson
mansion, which seems haunted by the presence of a long-dead
young girl, sixth grader Neely and her little brother become
regular visitors when emotionally disturbed Curtis Hutchinson
moves in.
ISBN 0-385-31055-2
[1. Ghosts—Fiction.   2. Emotional problems—Fiction.]   I. Title.
PZ7.S68522Tp   1994
[Fic]—dc20   93-31168
                                                              CIP
                                                              AC

Manufactured in the United States of America

August 1995

10   9   8   7

BVG

To Ben and Yvonne Lee
and especially to Michael and Jessica
with lots of love

CHAPTER

1

TOWARD THE END OF CORNELIA BRADFORD'S SIXTH-GRADE year at Carmel Middle School she wrote a very successful report for Mr. Hardcastle's language arts class. Mr. Hardcastle liked it a lot. When she got it back it had a large red *A* at the top of the page and beneath that the words, "Good for you, Neely. Well written and *fascinating* material. Particularly fascinating to me and to everyone in my core class this year." The title of her paper was "The Tragic Story of Halcyon House."

She began the report by explaining the origin of the word *halcyon*. "The word 'halcyon,'" she wrote, "originated in Greek mythology. In those olden days of ancient Greece, halcyons were believed to be seabirds who built their nests on the ocean waves. These beautiful birds were so beloved by the gods that during their nesting season the gods stilled the winds and waves so that their nests would not be disturbed. This is why the word 'halcyon' came to mean a time of beautiful peace and tranquility."

In the second paragraph of the report she began to tell about the history of Halcyon House itself. "And so," Neely had written, "in 1910 when Mr. Harold Hutchinson the first, an extremely wealthy businessman, built his magnificent mansion on the coast a few miles south of Carmel, he called it Halcyon House, because he hoped to find there the peace and beauty that he could not find anywhere else."

She didn't actually go into the fact that, according to rumor, old Harold the first had spent most of his life trampling all over anyone who happened to get in his way and that, along with his millions, he had earned an awful lot of hate and fear and jealousy—and not much peace and tranquility. But she did tell about some of the sad and tragic things that had happened to various members of the Hutchinson family in the years that followed. After admitting that most of the stories were based only on rumor, she told about the guest who had drowned in the swimming pool, the car accidents and serious illnesses—like pneumonia and alcoholism and insanity—that, over the years, had disturbed the tranquility of Halcyon House.

She finished the report by saying, "Now, once again, the Hutchinsons are gone from Halcyon. Harold Hutchinson's dream of the beautiful bird of peace is gone forever, and only a hawk haunts the wind that sweeps down Halcyon Hill."

She thought the ending, which was only slightly borrowed from her father's favorite poet, was especially good, and Mr. Hardcastle seemed to think so too. And he also mentioned that his whole core class would find the report particularly interesting, since they had all known a member of the Hutchinson family, if only for a very short time.

Of course, he was referring to Curtis, and of course, Neely hadn't said anything at all about Curtis in her report. She didn't mention Curtis or Monica and she certainly didn't mention some other facts that Mr. Hardcastle might have found particularly fascinating—the true facts about the strange and awful things that had happened at Halcyon House only a few months before.

So, even though "The Tragic Story of Halcyon House" earned a big red *A*, it certainly wasn't the whole story.

CHAPTER
2

IT ALL STARTED ON A MONDAY IN JUNE NOT LONG AFTER the beginning of summer vacation when Neely had just finished fifth grade. During breakfast that morning she noticed that her little brother, Grub (Gregory actually, but Grub to family and friends), was acting peculiarly, not eating anything and staring off into space with wide, unfocused eyes. She was just beginning to suspect that he was having another attack of what Aaron called Grubbie's sky-is-falling syndrome when Connie Bradford, their mother, looked up from writing on her calendar and told him to eat his scrambled eggs before they got cold.

"I can't, Mom," he said. "I can't eat them."

His mother erased something she'd just written, before she said, "Why not? What's wrong with them? They look perfectly all right to me."

Grub was staring down at the eggs as if he expected

them to leap off his plate and attack, like a small yellow version of the Blob. "Cholesterol," he whispered.

"Cholesterol?" Mom asked. "What do you know about cholesterol, Grubbie?" She got up to get some more coffee and came back to her chair. But when Grub just went on silently poking at his eggs, she said, "You know you'll just have to sit there until you finish your breakfast, don't you, dear? So you might as well get started." Then she tucked a strand of her long gray hair behind her ear, and went back to sipping her coffee and scribbling down notes about the things she had to get done that day.

Neely bit her lips, wanting to say, "Look at him, Mom. He's really working himself up again," but she didn't. It wouldn't have done any good. Instead she only said, "Grub, Mom asked you what you know about cholesterol."

Grub sighed and rolled his big, beautiful eyes tragically. "Everything," he said in a mournful tone of voice. "I read all about it in the *Times*."

He probably had too. Even though Grub was only eight-and-a-half years old he really could—and did—read everything, including the daily newspaper and the Encyclopedia Britannica. A fact which thrilled teachers and other intellectually inclined types like his father, but wasn't all that great really because a lot of what he read just gave him something else to worry about.

Just last week, for instance, he'd been certain that they were all about to be squashed by a falling meteorite, and before that it had been the disappearing rain forests. The rain forests thing had been a really major sky-is-falling at-tack—the kind that could last for days, and it was beginning to look as if this might be another. Unless something wonderful happened, like . . . Neely looked around, vaguely hoping for something wonderful to come to mind. Like, for instance, if the weather would just get better. Grub, who had always been strangely affected by the weather, usually was much easier to cheer up when the sun was shining.

But it was a typical June morning on the northern California coast—cold and damp, with a heavy ocean fog that was clearly going to hang on for hours. Not very good weather for moody types like Grub, that was for certain, but on the other hand it was a perfectly good day to stay indoors and read, which was exactly what Neely had been planning to do.

Grub was still staring at his eggs when Neely left the room. There wasn't anything she could do about it, so she put him out of her mind and went looking for the book about Joan of Arc that she'd just started reading the night before.

It was at least half an hour later, and Neely was curled up on the window seat in the living room, alternately reading and daydreaming, when Grub came in. She had just finished an excruciatingly tragic scene, and was busy imagining herself as Joan of Arc, calmly and courageously facing the English judges and then being led away to the stake, when Grub stumbled in and collapsed on the floor.

At first she tried to ignore him, but it wasn't easy. The way his arms and legs were flung out every which way made him look like the victim of some horrible disaster, and every few minutes he let out a long, pitiful sigh. She looked away and tried to bring back that tragic scene in the marketplace in Rouen, but it was no good. At last she gave up, put down her book, and asked Grub if he would like to do something. Like go for a walk, maybe.

Grub groaned again, rolled over on his back and looked at his watch before he said, "Well, all right. I guess I have time for a short walk."

"Time?" Neely asked. "Before what?"

Grub sighed. "Before I have a heart attack."

Neely got up, threw down her book, and yanked Grub to his feet. "Listen, Grubbie," she said. "If you don't shut up about your cholesterol, something's going to get attacked all right, but it won't be your heart. Come on. Let's go." Then she whacked him on his bottom and pulled him toward the door.

A few minutes later, as they were going down the back steps, Neely actually said—word for word—"Okay, which way shall we go? The ocean or the hills?" Which pretty much proved beyond a reasonable doubt that she started out that morning with absolutely no plans concerning Halcyon House. It was Grub who had chosen the hills—by way of the old Hutchinson Road, which, of course, passed right by the entrance to the estate—and Halcyon House.

CHAPTER
3

As they started up the hill it was obvious that, even though Grub had agreed to the walk, he hadn't agreed to cheer up. They passed the Jensens' property, with its great hedge of ancient cypresses, and went on up the steep slope that led to the top of the rise, with Grub trudging along silently, ignoring Neely's attempts to make conversation. After trying out several of his favorite conversational topics—such as his pets, word games, and the *meaning of life*, Neely more or less gave up and quit trying to get through to him. When they reached the top of the rise she stopped and turned toward the sea.

From there on the crest the land fell away in a long green slope. It leveled a little at the Bradfords' property and the highway beyond, but then it began to slope again. The green plain, covered with chaparral and brightened by splotches of lupine and Indian paintbrush, became steeper as it approached the sharp drop to where the waves crashed and foamed against the great gray rocks. And beyond that the Pacific Ocean stretched out everlastingly to meet and blend with the sky. Sometimes the view from the crest blazed with color—sea-blue, foam-white, and grass-green—brightened by clumps of red, yellow, and lavender. But today the drifting fog veiled both land and sea, fading everything into an endless dreary gray.

Stopping there on the crest to rest a moment and look down to the sea and listen for its distant roar had always been a part of any visit to the Halcyon Grove. Here, where a sloping boulder offered a thronelike seat, Neely had often stopped to sit, sometimes all by herself, but many other times on her way to the grove with Grub. Mostly just with Grub, but once in a while with their father, who sometimes came with them as far as the rocky throne. He always stopped there to recite poetry and tell stories about the early days on the Big Sur coast when only a few brave pioneer families had homesteaded on what some people called "the edge of the earth."

"Come on, Grub. Let's rest a minute." Neely scooted up onto her usual seat on the boulder. "Look. Look at the hawk. Look how . . ." She stopped, trying to remember a line from one of the Robinson Jeffers poems that Dad always quoted. "How does that poem go? The one about the air being haunted by hawks?"

Grub was usually interested in hawks and poetry, too, but today he only glanced up and then went plodding on. Sighing impatiently, she hurried after him and together they started down into the valley.

Below the crest the pavement ended and the road narrowed to a rutted and potholed lane. John Bradford, Grub and Neely's father, said that years ago the unpaved section was regularly graded and graveled, but that was when the original Harold Hutchinson was still alive and he and his family spent every summer in the mansion. For as long as Neely could remember, however, the road had been, as it was now, a narrow, weed-grown pathway that wound its way down into the heavily wooded valley.

On a bright, clear day Halcyon Grove was an enchanted place, its mysterious green-tinged shadows spangled with filtered sunlight, but today the light was dim and gray, and wisps of ocean fog drifted among the trees in ghostly veils. They walked silently down the steep slope among live oak and madrone trees and then into the deeper forest of redwoods and ponderosa pines that grew along the bed of the creek. Great towering trees that were native to the Monterey coast but which, in this particular place, had actually been planted years ago by gardeners so that the Hutchinsons could have their own private forest.

As they made their way through the dense grove Neely stole a glance now and then in her brother's direction to see if the old familiar magic was working. But today nothing seemed to help. Grub just went mooching along, his face puckered into a pug-nosed mask of tragedy.

For a moment Neely felt angry. Why should it always be her responsibility to cheer Grub up? After all, she was just his sister and only three years older than he was. But somehow it had always been more or less that way. She didn't know why exactly, except that she and Grub were a special case, being what some people called afterthought children and therefore almost like a separate family. After their parents had had Aaron and Julie and Lucinda, almost ten years had gone by before Neely was born, and then three years after that came the final afterthought, Gregory Bradford—or as Aaron called him when they brought him home from the hospital, "the Grub."

So maybe it was just that by the time Grubbie came along no one had the time or energy left to cope with things like his gloom-and-doom attacks. No one except Neely, and from time to time even she ran out of the kind of patience it took to deal with Grub's weird personality.

It did help, of course, that he was so gorgeous. If you're going to be a pain in the neck, it helps to be a beautiful one—though, of course, the opposite is true too. From very personal experience Neely knew that if you're not beautiful you'd better not be a nuisance—not if you know what's good for you.

If, for instance, you happened to inherit a square jaw and straight, no-particular-color hair instead of the fine features, masses of dark curls, and enormous long-lashed eyes of the Bradford side of the family, you really needed to work on your other talents. Talents such as poise and personality, which Neely apparently had plenty of, if poise and personality accounted for the fact that her classmates had elected her class president or secretary or treasurer more times than she could remember.

But having to make up for a lack in the appearance department was one problem Grub would never have to deal with. Even today, trudging along with his curly head bent down and a gloomy frown dipping the ends of his eyebrows and the corners of his lips, Grub somehow managed to look disgustingly charming. It really wasn't fair. Neely sighed and looked the other way.

They were climbing again on the far side of the valley where the road wound its way up toward the entrance to the Hutchinson estate, when Neely suddenly realized that Grub wasn't there beside her, nor anywhere on the road behind her—as if he had suddenly faded away into the drifting fog.

CHAPTER
4

FOR A MOMENT, LOOKING DOWN THE EMPTY FOG-DIMMED lane, Neely felt a twinge of anxiety, but she had barely started back the way they had come when she noticed a movement in the underbrush. And there, on the ground behind a tall clump of ferns, was Grub. Crouching down on his hands and knees, he seemed to be completely engrossed in something on the ground in front of him.

Good, Neely thought. Grub had always been so fascinated by every kind of living thing that sometimes all it took to cure one of his depressions was an unusual bug, or butterfly, or even a particularly gruesome slug. All prepared to make an enthusiastic fuss over whatever it was he'd found—*Wow! Look at that! Isn't that the most beautiful . . . or interesting . . . or slimiest . . . or whatever seemed appropriate*—she hurried over to squat down beside him—and immediately realized that what Grub had found this time wasn't going to help at all. It was a tiny baby squirrel. A tiny *dead* baby squirrel. And *death* had been high on Grub's anxiety list since he was about four years old, when he'd started asking everyone to explain death, and tell him why God allowed it to happen.

Reaching out with one finger, Grub touched the tiny furry head between its pitiful little sunken eyes and then looked up at Neely.

"Why?" he said in a quavering voice. "Why did it have to die, Neely?"

"Look, Grub." Neely knew she was sounding exasperated but she couldn't help it. The "why death" question was one Grub had pestered her with for so long she'd pretty much run out of answers. "I've told you before, and so have Mom and Dad, that there's just no point in—"

But at that very moment she heard something that made her lose track of what she was saying . . . the nearby stutter and chug of an approaching car. Crouching down beside Grub she whispered, "Shhh. Get down. It's Reuben."

Peering through the ferns, they watched as a rusty old pickup truck struggled around the curve, weaving from side to side as it bounced in and out of the deep ruts. Inside the cab a slouching figure topped by a floppy old hat was just visible through the dusty window. It was Reuben all right, on his way to the highway on his regular Monday trip to Monterey.

Reuben Flores, who lived in a small cabin behind the main house at Halcyon, had been the watchman and caretaker of the Hutchinson property for as long as Neely could remember. His dog, a very large mastiff called Lion, was, according to rumor, attack trained and a vicious man-killer. Whenever Reuben left Halcyon, which he did every Monday and usually on Saturdays, too, he turned Lion loose to roam the estate grounds. Which meant that no one—no local kids and not even any nosy tourists—dared so much as set foot on the Hutchinson property. No one dared, that is, except Grub and Neely Bradford, who had been regular visitors to the grounds of Halcyon House for almost two years.

Grub had been only six years old at the time of their first visit to the estate grounds. On that particular day he and Neely had been playing a game in the grove. The game, if Neely remembered correctly, had been based on *The Jungle Book*, which was one of their favorites that year. Grub, as Mowgli, had run off pretending to be kidnapped by the Bandar Log. But when Neely, playing the part of Bagheera, the black panther, went to the rescue, Grub wasn't in any of their regular hiding places.

She had looked everywhere and was getting a little frantic when she heard a giggle coming from the other side of the huge wrought iron fence that surrounded the estate grounds. And there she had finally found Grub, sitting on the ground in the middle of the Hutchinsons' weed-grown driveway, being enthusiastically slobbered over by the terrible Lion. Lion, it seemed, like almost every other animal Grub had ever met, had fallen in love with him at first sight.

After that amazing discovery they had returned many times to visit Lion—and the grounds of the estate. All they had to do was watch and listen for Reuben's pickup as it chugged past their house, and they would be off, up the hill, down into the grove, and from there into the estate grounds. Then, with Lion trotting happily along beside them, they would explore the weed-grown lawns and gardens, the crumbling tennis court, the grand old stable with its high-domed hayloft, and even walk along the leaf-strewn verandas of the huge house, trying to peek in through the shuttered windows.

Neely was particularly fascinated by the windows. Windows of deserted houses, she had always thought, were like sad, empty eyes, forever weeping invisible tears for the warmth and life they had once known. And the windows of Halcyon House were particularly spellbinding because of all the strange things she had heard about the people who had once lived within its walls.

But it was impossible to see very much through the cracks in the heavy old shutters. So the secrets of Halcyon House remained hidden away. Hidden, that is, until that day. The day of Grub's cholesterol anxiety attack.

CHAPTER
5

NEELY WAITED UNTIL REUBEN HAD COMPLETELY DIS-
appeared into the fog before she crawled out from behind
the ferns. Standing in the middle of the road, she looked
back to where her brother was again staring mournfully at
the dead squirrel. "Come on, Grub," she said suddenly.
"Let's go." She didn't have to say where.

Grub gave the dead squirrel one last lingering glance,
got to his feet, and without a word led the way into the
estate grounds. Not, of course, by way of the grand gateway
where wrought iron vines twisted up sturdy pillars and
formed themselves into an archway of ornate letters spell-
ing the word *Halcyon*. Passing by the gate, which as always
was locked and chained and doubly padlocked, they went
on up the slope to where a dense thicket of Scotch broom
grew up on both sides of the fence. There, in the midst of
the thicket, a socket had rusted out, so one of the iron fence
poles could be pushed to one side, leaving a sizable gap. A

gap through which Grub had crawled on that first day when he discovered that Lion was really a pussycat—and through which he, and Neely as well, had crept many times since.

Inside the fence they zigzagged through the weeds, tip-toeing carefully and as lightly as possible to avoid establishing a telltale path to their secret entrance. But once on the driveway they needed only to follow the deep ruts worn by Reuben's pickup. The road rose steeply here as it curved and twisted through a grove of ornamental trees and bushes, ending on the high plateau from which Halcyon House had looked down for more than eighty years . . . down over the narrow wooded valley that cut through the treeless plain and on out to the endless blue of sea and sky. They had just reached the plateau when Lion emerged from behind the house and bounded out to meet them.

Grub's giggle sounded almost normal when Lion showered him with sloppy kisses, and later when they discovered the tadpoles in the stagnant water of the swimming pool, his behavior certainly seemed to be typical Grubbiness. Squatting at the water's edge, he stared at the bug-eyed black blobs in the slimy green water with the kind of concentration that most kids save for their favorite TV programs. Watching Grub watch the tadpoles, Neely decided the sky-is-falling syndrome was over, at least for the time being, which was a decided relief.

After the tadpoles finally lost their charm, they moved on past Reuben's tiny cottage and Lion's enormous dog-house, and then through the rose garden, to pay a visit to the stable. The beautiful old stable, built in the same massive rustic style as the house itself, was one of Neely's favorite places and a visit there was always included when she and Grub visited the grounds of Halcyon.

They entered the stable by the small door set into one of the large double panels that had once opened to accommodate wagons or trucks. Once inside it was necessary to wait for a few moments while their eyes accustomed themselves to the dim light before they could move forward over the dusty inlaid brick floor. Neely loved walking down the central corridor sniffing carefully for the faint faraway odor of hay and horse and imagining beautiful Thoroughbred and Arabian heads sticking out over the doors of the roomy box stalls on either side.

Leaving the stables, they moved on slowly across the weed-grown lawns, pushed their way through the trailing tentacles of vine in the sagging grape arbor, and then came back to rest on a stone bench at the edge of what had once been a rose garden.

The bench faced the south wing of the house, where an ancient wisteria vine coiled around the stone pillars that supported the roof of the veranda. From that angle, facing away from the weed-grown lawns and gardens, the house, seen by itself, still looked grand and imposing. The lower level with its walls and pillars of gray fieldstone looked as if it would last forever, and even the upper floors with their heavy wooden shingles seemed almost untouched by time. It was only the peeling paint on door and window frames and a few sagging shutters that spoiled the illusion. But if Neely squinted her eyes only a little, the house looked almost as magnificent as it must have during its days of glory.

She often thought about those olden days at Halcyon House.

"Dad says there were parties here all the time," she told Grub, "with people going up our road in fancy cars with chauffeurs in uniforms."

Grub's eyes were unfocused. "And carriages with lots of white horses."

Neely laughed. "No, silly. Dad's not that old. And the house isn't that old. Dad says it was built in 1910, and there were already cars by then. And by the time Dad can remember, there were lots of cars."

Grub shrugged. "There were carriages once, with white horses. I read all about it in the encyclopedia."

He hadn't, of course. Anytime Grub wanted to win an argument he claimed to have read about it in the encyclopedia. But Neely didn't ask him if he was telling the truth. She and Grub had always had a kind of silent agreement about certain kinds of questions. The agreement was that they didn't ask questions about whether something was "really true" or not. "Really true" questions were absolutely out. And besides, she rather liked the thought of the horse-drawn carriages herself.

She was still imagining the horses when Grub asked, "Why did they all go away?"

"You know why," Neely said. "Dad told us. And I've told you before. Lots of times."

"I know, but I want to hear it again. I want to hear it now, while I'm looking at the house."

That made sense. Neely was sure she could tell it better while the grand old house was right there in front of her.

"Well," she began. "The first Harold Hutchinson was a very rich man. The richest man in the whole world." She wasn't sure about that last part, but it did make the story more exciting. She could tell that Grub liked it, too, so she added some more.

"He was so rich that he had dozens of houses all over the world. So many houses that some of them he only lived in for three or four days out of the whole year. He had grand palaces in Europe and everywhere and when he was going to visit them a whole army of servants would come first and clean everything up and put flowers in all the rooms. And then the Hutchinsons would come roaring up in huge silver Rolls-Royces, with all their friends and relations, and they'd stay for two or three days and then they'd go away for another year."

That part of the story was mostly new, but Neely was really sure about the next part because she'd heard her dad say so. "But Harold Hutchinson the First loved Halcyon the best of all his houses, and as long as he was alive all his family, and a lot of relatives and friends, too, came here every year and stayed all through the summer."

"But why did they stop coming?"

"Well, Dad says it was partly because they weren't so rich anymore. Dad says after the first Harold died, Harold the Second was better at spending money than at making it. So maybe they just couldn't afford to come anymore. But that's just part of it. The other part of it was"—Neely paused and widened her eyes—"the other part was because the Hutchinsons were star-crossed."

21

CHAPTER

6

"TELL ABOUT WHAT HAPPENS WHEN YOU'RE STAR-crossed," Grub said.

Neely had to stop to think for a moment. But then she remembered where she'd heard it—about the Hutchinsons being star-crossed. It had been Greta Peale who called them that. Greta Peale, an old lady who had lived on the coast all her life, was one of the Bradfords' nearest neighbors and once, a long time ago, Neely had overheard Greta telling her mom about the star-crossed Hutchinsons.

"A long time ago," she told Grub, "I heard Greta telling Mom how the Hutchinsons were star-crossed and that was why all these terrible things happened at Halcyon House. I asked Mom about it afterward and she said it was nonsense. She said it was just more of Greta's gossip."

"What does *star-crossed* mean?" Grub asked.

Neely nodded. "I looked it up. The dictionary said ill-fated and, like, cursed. It said, like star-crossed people had a curse on them."

"What kind of curses happen when you're star-crossed?"

Neely wasn't sure. Greta and Mom had lowered their voices when they noticed Neely was listening. But she had heard a little bit and she'd guessed some more. "Oh, like horrible accidents, like car accidents and drownings. And people getting sick and dying," she told Grub. "And there was this little girl who died in the house. So after a while most of the Hutchinsons quit coming to Halcyon. But they couldn't just sell it because the first Harold had it put in his will that Halcyon could never be sold, no matter what."

"I know," Grub said impatiently. "I know all that stuff about the will. You told me that before."

Neely shook her head slowly. Grub could be so exasperating. "I know you know it, but you asked. Why did you ask if you didn't want me to tell you?"

Grub looked surprised. "Because I thought you might tell some new parts."

"But I don't know any other parts. That's it. That's all I ever heard about it."

"I know. But sometimes you put in some new things. I mean besides what you heard."

Neely knew what he meant, of course. Like the part about Harold Hutchinson the First being the richest man in the world. What Grub meant was he liked it when she thought up exciting new details. She was considering one or two more when Grub asked, "That little girl who died. Why did she die?"

Neely looked at him quickly, fearing the worst. But this time Grub didn't seem to be in a "why death" mood. At least not yet.

"I mean," Grub said, "what made her die? Was it some terrible disease like diphtheria? I read about diphtheria in—"

"I know," Neely said. "You read about it in the encyclopedia." They grinned at each other. "I don't know what she . . ." Neely stopped. "Well, actually," she went on more slowly—and much more dramatically. "Nobody ever really knew. It was like she . . . suddenly disappeared. Or at least that was what people said. One day . . . well, one minute she was right there, playing in her room and then suddenly she was gone. And no one ever saw her again."

Grub nodded slowly, his eyes as blank and unfocused as a sleepwalker's. Neely watched him, grinning inwardly. "Suddenly she was gone," he said dreamily, "and no one ever saw her again." He looked around the rose garden and then on up to the second-story windows. He stared at the windows for a while before he turned back to Neely. "I think that was her room," he said. "That little window there at the end, but after that terrible day no one ever saw her—"

But at that moment the dreamy smile faded and Grub's face stiffened. Following his gaze, Neely saw a gray squirrel running across the weed-choked lawn. "It's the mother," Grub said, and then went on whispering so softly that she couldn't quite hear. But she could guess. From the expression on Grub's face she could guess that he was telling himself that this squirrel was the heartbroken mother of the dead baby.

The squirrel seemed to be scouting around at the edge of what had once been lawn as if it were looking for something. Grub stared at it for a long time.

"She's looking for her baby," he whispered finally in a quivering voice, "but she'll never see him again."

"Grub," Neely said firmly, "she—or he probably—is looking for acorns. Forget it. Besides, I haven't finished telling you about the girl who disappeared." She glanced around, looking frantically for inspiration, and her eyes fell on the corner window above the veranda. "What I wanted to tell you was that you guessed right. That was her room, right up there on the end, and . . ."

That was when she noticed something very interesting. "And you know what?" she went on. "I'll bet we could go up there and peek right in her window and see what her room looked like."

What Neely had noticed was that the upstairs windows, with their open shutters, could easily be reached from the veranda roof. By standing on the roof you could . . . She'd gotten that far in her reasoning when she noticed that it was already working—Grub seemed to have stopped mourning over the grief-stricken mother squirrel and was staring at the upstairs window. "But how do we get up there on the veranda?" he asked.

Neely looked around and almost immediately found the answer. At the end of the veranda the trunk of the old wisteria vine, thick and heavy as a man's arm, curled and curved its way upward around the corner pillar. "The vine," she told Grub. "We climb right up the vine—just like Mowgli."

Grub nodded. "Or Tarzan. We climb up the vine like Tarzan." He got up off the bench and started toward the house so quickly that Neely had to run to catch up.

The climb was easy. The lower part of the vine was as simple to climb as a ladder. The only problem was near the top where the branches were thinner and tended to bend a little under Neely's weight. But by careful placing of her hands and feet she managed to slither her way up over the eaves. And right behind her Grub, who was much lighter, came up as quick and easy as a monkey. And then they were both standing on the thick old roof shingles looking down to where Lion sat staring up at them with a puzzled look on his big saggy-jawed face.

Grub giggled, and Neely, congratulating herself on her successful sky-is-falling cure, began to make her way over the slippery moss-covered shingles toward the corner window. She had reached the window and was kneeling in front of it, trying to peer through the dirty glass, when she heard Grub say, "Look, Neely. It's not closed. The window isn't all the way closed."

CHAPTER
7

AT FIRST THE WINDOW REFUSED TO BUDGE. IT SEEMED TO be jammed in place as firmly as if the wood of window and frame had grown together. Neely pulled and tugged without any success at all, until she thought of pounding on the frame with the heel of her shoe to jar it free. After that she began to make some slow progress. When the opening was nearly wide enough to squeeze through, she sat back on her heels and looked at Grub.

"Maybe we shouldn't . . ." she started to say, and stopped. And to be honest, she probably didn't mean it. To be absolutely honest, at that very minute, probably nothing short of the arrival of a half dozen police cars with screeching sirens could have stopped her from crawling through that window into Halcyon House. Particularly after she noticed the expression on Grub's face. He looked excited, and even more important, positively cheerful. Not a trace of sky-is-falling syndrome. So that decided it. Neely put her head and arms through the opening, reached down and touched the floor. Walking her hands forward, she pulled and wiggled until she landed in a heap—and got quickly to her feet.

The large room was dim and shadowy. The fog-faded light, entering through two dirt-encrusted windows, seemed to be almost totally absorbed by the dark wood paneling of the surrounding walls. As her eyes became accustomed to the semidarkness Neely was able to see a fancy dressing table, a marble-topped dresser, and a large old-fashioned bed shaped like a sleigh. The sleek dark wood of the bed's head and foot gleamed elegantly even through a thick layer of dust. Near a small fireplace there were two upholstered chairs, draped with sheets. The air smelled old and dead. Neely's shoulders lifted in a sharp shiver.

"Look," she heard Grub say. "Here's some of her clothing."

Neely's breath caught in a quick gasp. She turned quickly but Grub was nowhere in sight. Then she noticed an open closet door and there he was bending over a large pile of what seemed to be old, faded rags. Dust flew as he lifted a ruffled blouse yellowed with age.

"Don't," Neely said sharply. "Don't touch it." She took the blouse away, pulled Grub out of the closet, and closed the door. He moved on around the room, humming softly to himself, examining each piece of furniture closely before moving on to the next. Neely particularly noticed the humming because it was something Grub always did when he was feeling especially good. Near the door he stopped to try the old-fashioned light switch that turned from side to side.

Nothing happened. The chandelier, as well as the fancy wall lamps shaped like torches, stayed dark. "I guess it's broken," he said.

"Or turned off," Neely said. "The electricity is probably turned off."

He nodded and went on exploring and Neely went on watching him. He looked excited, she decided, but not frightened. Grub didn't seem to be at all frightened. Neely was still standing motionless in the center of the room when he came back to her and looked up into her face.

"What's wrong?" he asked.

"I don't know," Neely said. "I guess I just feel strange about being here."

Grub's eyes were untroubled, clear and wide. "Why?"

"I don't know. Because we'd be in trouble if we were caught in here, I guess. What if Reuben came back early for some reason and came in and caught us?" She looked around uneasily before she went on. "But it's not just Reuben. It's like maybe . . . something else doesn't want us to be here."

Grubb nodded slowly. Then he turned to look around the room, his head cocked as if he were listening. At last he turned back to Neely. "It's all right," he said. "I think it's all right. Come on. I want to see everything." He headed toward the door.

"Wait." Neely grabbed his arm and pulled him back and together they moved slowly forward.

The door was of dark wood like the paneling. Large and heavy, it had a central panel deeply carved in what seemed to be a native design, perhaps Indian or Eskimo. The doorknob, bronze colored and intricately etched, felt heavy and solid under her hand. Neely turned it slowly and, still grasping Grub's arm, stepped out into a dim hallway. For a long moment she stood very still listening.

"Neely?" Grub whispered.

"Shhh," she said.

"What is it? What do you hear?"

Neely shook her head. She didn't know what she was listening for, or why she felt so certain that she could hear it if she listened hard enough. "I don't know," she whispered. "I just feel like someone might be here."

CHAPTER

8

SHE HADN'T MEANT TO SAY IT. SHE HADN'T MEANT TO SAY out loud what she had been thinking and feeling—that someone or something else might be in the house with them. It seemed that saying it might make it true, or at least a lot more frightening. But somehow it had slipped out.

"Umm," Grub said. He cocked his head again and listened and then looked up and down the hall before he nodded slowly. "Come on, Neely," he said. "Let's look."

There was a rug on the floor, a long runner with an Indian pattern of triangles and diamonds and zigzag lines. The walls were wood paneled halfway up and above the paneling there was a heavy fabric that looked and felt like tightly woven reeds. The smooth hardwood floor on each side of the rug was covered with dust. A *thin* smooth layer of grayish powder.

"Someone's been here," Neely whispered. "Not too long ago. I mean, there's dust but not like it would be if no one had been here for twenty or thirty years." She stopped and ran her finger along the ledge at the top of the paneling. "See?"

"Maybe it's Reuben," Grub said. "Maybe Reuben comes in and cleans."

Neely nodded. Why hadn't she thought of that? Probably Reuben did come in to clean. The idea that someone had been taking care of the house, that it hadn't been sitting empty and alone for all those years, was somehow a little bit comforting. Taking Grub's hand, she moved on down the hall.

The other bedrooms on the second floor were also furnished with heavy old-fashioned furniture. Some had beds with high wooden headboards and marble-topped dressers while others were less formal with brass beds and white wicker chairs. Some of the rooms had small things in them, too—pictures on the walls, clocks, vases, hand mirrors, crystal jars and bottles—but others were empty except for a few big pieces of furniture. There were several large bathrooms with old-fashioned claw-foot tubs, pull-chain toilets, and pedestal basins.

As they went from room to room Neely gradually began to feel a little better—more excited instead of scared. She couldn't help feeling thrilled over all the beautiful old rooms with their paneled walls and lead-paned windows. So many rooms full of such beautiful things.

But once or twice the quick pulse of fear came again like a faint faraway warning when she first stepped into a new room. And with the fear the strong feeling that there were sounds around her that she could hear if only she could listen hard enough.

At the south end of the hall Grub discovered a locked door. As he twisted the knob back and forth and then tried to peek through the keyhole Neely began to feel it again, a strange uneasy tension that made a tingle at the back of her neck and a tight stretched feeling across her face.

"Don't do that, Grub," she said.

"But it's locked. Why do you suppose it's locked, Neely?"

"I don't know. Maybe there's something valuable in there. Maybe jewelry or bottles of expensive old wine."

Grub shook his head and tried again to look through the keyhole.

"Stop it, Grub," Neely said sharply.

"Why?" he said. "Why not?"

"Because . . ." She didn't know "why not" exactly, except that it made her feel uneasy. "Because it's none of your business."

Grub was still staring at the door. "But maybe that's where the secret is," he said.

"What secret?"

"The secret about the girl who disappeared."

Neely smiled. "You mean, you think she's in there. Her bones or something. She disappeared a long time ago. Like before Dad was born even." It was a ridiculous idea, and Neely didn't even want to imagine about it.

Grub shrugged. "Not her bones. Just something about her secret, maybe."

Neely grabbed his arm and pulled him away.

In the center portion of the long hall a staircase led up to the third floor and down to the first. The stairs to the first floor were very wide with a great solid banister almost a foot across. The stairway ended in a grand entryway facing some ornate double doors, which Neely immediately recognized. She'd seen the massive entry doors many times before—from the outside.

In the downstairs rooms the bottom sections of the tall windows were shuttered, so the only light came in through small arched upper panes. A dim light, but enough to see that the living room was very long and grand with a beamed ceiling, an enormous fireplace, huge leather couches and chairs, and lots of other bulky-looking pieces of furniture.

There were paintings on the walls, too, seascapes and still lifes, and over the mantel a large painting of a stern-faced old man wearing an old-fashioned suit and a shirt with a high stiff collar.

In a corner near the windows there was a potted tree that reached almost to the ceiling. Its limbs were dry and bare and the floor beneath it was covered with dead leaves. Grub stared at the tree, his forehead puckering.

"I guess Reuben doesn't come in here very often," Neely said. "At least, not often enough for that poor tree."

"Could we water it?" Grub asked.

"It wouldn't do any good. It's been dead too long," Neely said—and bit her tongue. *Dead* wasn't a good word to use around Grub, not even about a tree. But this time his mind seemed to be busy elsewhere.

After the living room they explored the dining room, kitchen, and a lot of small rooms—pantries, storage rooms, and what seemed to be several small bedrooms, probably for servants. The pantries were empty except for mouse droppings and long ribbons of spiderweb that draped down from shelf to shelf.

In the enormous kitchen the appliances were large and grand and very old-fashioned. Grub kept opening cupboards and closets even though Neely told him not to. There were dishes and pots and pans in some of the cupboards, as if people had gone away planning to come back very soon, and for some reason had never returned.

When they'd finished exploring the north wing of the house they went back through the entryway and into a large game room. Two beautiful game tables of inlaid wood sat near the windows, and in the center of the room a huge stained glass chandelier hung down over a pool table with bulging carved legs and pockets with golden tassels.

Beyond the game room there was a library with comfortable chairs and couches and lots of bookshelves that went clear up to the ceiling. Most of the shelves were still filled with books—old, dusty books with dark, discolored bindings.

Over the fireplace in the library there was another large oil painting, this time of a group of people—a family, probably. A handsome man with a mustache and slicked-down dark hair and a sad-looking woman wearing a pearl necklace and a dark dress with a long, tight skirt. There were also three children in the picture. Two half-grown boys and a pretty little girl with a big ribbon in her long curly hair. Grub studied the picture for so long that Neely finally had to pull him away.

CHAPTER
9

After the library Neely led the way back to the second floor and headed for the room with the open window. "Come on," she whispered. "Let's go home." But Grub didn't want to leave.

"We haven't been up there yet," he said, pointing to the flight of stairs that led up to the third floor.

Neely stopped, staring up at where, in the dim light of a stained glass skylight, the stairs turned and disappeared from view. She felt torn. One half of her wanted very much to see the whole house while they were there—all of it—but on the other hand . . .

The weird feeling of dread had almost gone away while they were in the library, but now, as they climbed the stairs, she could feel it oozing out from the dark corners of her mind. Oozing out and spreading like the strange tinted shadows that fell down across the stairwell from the stained glass skylight—yellow shadows and green ones, and one dull red blot that splashed across the landing like an old faded stain. She stopped and stood stiffly, staring at the red blot—and then suddenly turned back. Back down the stairs toward the room with the open window and the clean, fresh air of the outdoors. But by then Grub was almost to the top of the stairs and when she called him he didn't stop. So she turned again and followed him up the stairs.

The landing at the top of the stairs opened into one huge room, a kind of ballroom. An enormous open space with slanted ceilings, dormer windows, and a smooth hardwood floor. Along the walls were couches and chairs and on one side of the room there was a player piano and on the other an old-fashioned hand-cranked phonograph. Grub turned the handle and then took a record from the cabinet and put it on the turntable.

"It's all right," he said. "I won't hurt it. I know how. The man at the discovery museum showed me how to work one just like it."

He lifted the arm and lowered the needle carefully onto the edge of the record. It was piano music, tinny and jazzy-sounding. When it was over Grub wanted to play some others, but Neely was feeling more and more anxious.

"We'd better go," she said. "Reuben really might come back early."

It wasn't likely. On Mondays Reuben always stayed all day when he went into town. But there was always the possibility that he could change his routine. And besides, they'd been in the house for a long time. *And* Neely's urge to leave—to walk swiftly downstairs—perhaps even to run—was getting stronger and stronger.

"Okay," Grub said. "I just want to look at the drums. There on the stage. Come on."

At the far end of the room there was what certainly did look like a small stage. Probably a bandstand, Neely thought, where the musicians sat for the grand dances Dad talked about. While Grub, humming again, examined a decrepit old set of drums, Neely stood on the bandstand imagining the long narrow floor crowded with dancers, the women in long velvet or satin dresses and the men in fancy tuxedos. And the band—a big one with lots of blaring trumpets and wailing saxophones. Still imagining the band, she turned and, for the first time, noticed the view from the window.

The window was long and low and had a wide sill. The lower half of the glass pane was protected by two strong metal bars, but above the bars nothing obstructed a view that went on forever. Here, just beyond the northern end of the house, the plateau ended in a steep, rocky cliff. Far below lay the treeless plain and even farther away to the northeast the dim blue line where the ocean met the sky. It was a beautiful scene—the sloping green plain splashed with yellow and red, and farther away the blue-green sea spangled with sunlight.

"Look, Grub." She grabbed his arm and pulled him away from the drums. "Look. The sun's come out. And look at the view."

For a moment Grub looked, but then he suddenly stepped back, pushing himself away from Neely and the windowsill. At the edge of the stage he turned back, frowning.

"What's the matter?" Neely asked.

He shrugged. "I don't know. I just don't like looking down there."

Neely looked out the window again, seeing this time not the distant view to the plain and the sea, but what could be seen if you looked straight down. Straight down the three stories of Halcyon House and then the long steep drop of the plateau wall. She shivered, and then turned back to look at Grub.

"It's all right," she said. "See the bars. No one could possibly fall out."

"Umm." Grub nodded, but his forehead was still wrinkled. He turned away and started walking down the long room. Halfway to the door he turned back and said over his shoulder, "Let's go now, Neely. Let's go home."

CHAPTER

10

WHEN NEELY CLIMBED OUT ONTO THE VERANDA ROOF AND shut the window behind her it was with a definite feeling of relief. The kind of jittery mixture of relief and satisfaction that you feel when you're being unbuckled from a really terrifying carnival ride. Exactly the kind of "I'm glad I did it—but *never* again" reaction she'd had when she climbed out of the loop-the-loop at the fairgrounds.

But on the way home the jittery feeling gradually faded and was replaced by a pleasant excitement as she conjured up memory pictures of everything she had seen. All the great old rooms came back vividly—and with each scene she imagined interesting additions.

In the dining room she added to the memory of paneled walls and elegant furniture the image of an old man seated at the end of the table. An old man with a stern face and a great bush of gray hair. And other diners, men and women in beautiful clothing and among them a lovely slender woman and three children.

In her imagined scene the boys, dressed in grown-up–looking suits like the ones they were wearing in the portrait, were acting like kids, poking each other and grinning —probably about the silly things the grown-ups were saying. They had looked that way in the picture, as she recalled, a little bit devilish with their long sleek faces and tilted eyebrows. And then there was the little girl in her lacy dress and huge hair ribbon, looking very beautiful with her masses of curly hair and huge solemn eyes.

She kept playing around with the imagined scenes the rest of the day, even while she was sweeping the porches and helping Mom weed the garden. Grub helped with the weeding, too, for a little while, humming softly to himself as he worked. That is, until he found a tomato worm and went off to take it to a safe place where it wouldn't have to be squashed. After he'd gone Mom mentioned the humming.

"Well," she said, "I must say your hike to the grove was a grand success, Neely. I thought we were in for a bad case of blues this time. Cholesterol blues."

"Yes," Neely agreed. "Grub likes to hike." Which was certainly true, as far as it went.

That night in bed the half-remembered, half-imagined pictures came back even more vividly. But then as she began to drift toward sleep the pictures faded and left behind a puzzling question.

It was a double question. Part of it was about why she had felt so uneasy in Halcyon House, and the other part was why Grub hadn't. At least, he hadn't except for that moment near the window—which was probably just because he'd never liked high places. Why did she, Neely Bradford, who was seldom frightened of anything, feel almost terrified at times? And why was little old Grub, who was afraid of almost everything unless it had fur or feathers, so much at ease? She was wondering sleepily if it would be the same next time when suddenly she came wide awake. Next time. But of course there wasn't going to be a next time.

There wouldn't be any next time because it was too dangerous. Dangerous, she felt certain, in a lot of ways—some of which she couldn't really put into words. But the one danger that was easy to explain was Reuben. Reuben might just happen to come home early, or she and Grub might have left footprints or some other clue that would warn him—and so he might come back early on purpose to catch the intruder.

She imagined the capture, with the sour-faced old man springing out at them from behind a door and then dragging them away to the police station in his pickup truck.

And then the scene in the station in which she would try desperately to explain that they were not really guilty of breaking and entering because climbing in the window at Halcyon House had been entirely unpremeditated and had only happened because of Grub's cholesterol anxiety attack.

"I, Cornelia Emily Bradford, plead not guilty," she

would say. "We both plead not guilty. Because we didn't mean to, and we're sorry, and we won't ever do it again."

She meant it too. That night when Neely imagined herself promising never again to set foot inside Halcyon House, she really meant what she said.

CHAPTER
11

AFTER THAT FIRST VISIT TO HALCYON HOUSE EVERYTHING returned to normal. Summer vacation normal, that is—peaceful and quiet and more or less boring. On Tuesday Grub started spending most of his time in the chicken shed because his banty hen was hatching some baby chicks. The chicks were something to see, all right—cocky little fluff balls hardly bigger than bumblebees. And Grub, sitting there cross-legged on the floor in a baby-chick trance, was something to see too. Since there wasn't much going on anywhere else, Neely went out now and then to check on the action in the chicken shed, such as it was.

On Wednesday things got a little more exciting. Neely talked Dad into letting her ride into Carmel with him when he went to work at the motel. While Dad took over for the Martins (Sam and Betty Martin were the managers of Dad's motel in Carmel), Neely spent the day with her friend, Mimi Page. She and Mimi went to the beach and to Harrison Library, and she came home that night with a slight sunburn and a bunch of library books. Staggering into the house carrying a huge load of new library books was always a good feeling.

That evening she sat on the front steps and read until it got too dark and then watched the sunset over the ocean and thought first about the day with Mimi and then about Halcyon House.

She would have loved to tell Mimi about going inside the old mansion—Mimi, who loved mysterious things, would have absolutely freaked. But, of course, she didn't tell. A long time ago when she and Grub first began going onto the grounds at Halcyon they'd solemnly promised each other that they would *never* tell anyone. And not telling was even more important now that they'd actually been inside the house.

Inside Halcyon House. Sometimes she could hardly believe it had happened. But now that it was over and done with and nothing terrible had happened she was extremely glad she'd opened that window and climbed in. Because now she would always have all those great memory-pictures to add to her Halcyon House daydreams.

As she sat there on the porch that evening, it occurred to Neely that the summer was getting off to a good start. The fog had disappeared, she and Mimi had made some interesting plans, and down on Highway One what seemed to be a record number of summer tourists were already pouring up and down the coast.

That was good, too, because that meant lots of business for the Sea Mist Motel, and *that* meant less money problems for the Bradford family, at least for a while. People who lived on the coast usually got awfully sick of summer tourists, but that particular evening Neely even felt good about all the BMWs and Jeep Cherokees tooling up and down Highway One. But, as it happened, it was the very next morning that one of the summer tourists ran over Robinson.

Robinson was, or had been, a cat. A tall, gray, sad-eyed cat, and out of all Grub's pets probably the one he loved the most. He had been named Robinson because of a framed photo Dad had of his favorite poet, Robinson Jeffers. Grub seemed to think his cat and Robinson Jeffers looked a lot alike.

Neely had been in the kitchen getting a snack that morning when Dad came in the back door carrying a cardboard box. One look at Dad's face told her something was terribly wrong. But before she could even ask what had happened, Grub came into the kitchen too.

"Dad?" Grub asked immediately, and then winced as if he were expecting something to smash into his face.

"Grubbie," Dad said. "It's Robinson. He's—he's been hit by a car. I'm afraid he's dead, son."

Grub's head jerked around away from Dad and the box, but then he looked back at it out of the corners of his eyes. He just stood there like that for a while, staring sideways at the box and taking long shaky breaths. Then, in a high, tight voice, he said, "Is Robinson . . . in there?" When Dad nodded Grub shook his head and kept shaking it. "No," he kept saying. "No. He's not dead. He's not.

Maybe he's just unconscious. Dad, couldn't he just be unconscious?"

"No, Grubbie." Dad's voice sounded almost as close to tears as Grub's. "No. He's dead, son."

Then Grub turned around and ran. The door of his room slammed, and Neely, who had started to run after him, heard the key turn in the lock. When she knocked and rattled the doorknob there was no answer.

CHAPTER
12

GRUB STAYED IN HIS ROOM ALL DAY AND WOULDN'T LET anyone come in. Mom and Dad took turns trying to talk to him through the door, but he wouldn't answer except to say he was all right. Neely tried, too, several times, and all he would say was, "Go away, Neely."

Finally, after making some plans and gathering up the things she would need, she went back and knocked on his door again and said, "Grub, I'm going to have a funeral for Robinson. I have the stuff all ready to make him this big, beautiful tombstone with his picture on it, but I can't decide where to dig the grave. Do you think you could come help me pick a good place?"

There was a long moment of silence and then the sound of the key turning in the lock. The door opened slowly. Grub's eyes were red and his thick dark eyelashes were stuck together in long pointy clumps. He turned away, hiding his face.

"Neely," he said. "Don't have the funeral today. Wait till tomorrow. I'll help with it tomorrow—if he's . . ."

Neely caught her breath, fighting a sharp ache in the center of her chest. It hurt so much, she wanted to curl up around it in a tight knot, but she knew that wouldn't make it any better. The pain was from knowing Grub still hadn't given up hoping that Robinson wasn't really dead.

For a moment she couldn't say anything and even when she could speak she couldn't make herself say what ought to be said. She couldn't tell Grub there wasn't the slightest chance that Robinson was still alive. Instead she just said, "All right. I won't have the funeral until tomorrow then. We can have it tomorrow. Okay?"

Before she left the room, she hugged him while he stood stiff and still with his face turned away from her. Out in the hall she leaned against the wall and wished she'd said a lot of things she hadn't. She wished she'd told him to stop hoping that Robinson was still alive because he wasn't, and to go on pretending that he might be was just dragging out the pain. She stood there for quite a while wondering if she should go back in and tell him it was hopeless, but she couldn't bring herself to do it. Finally she decided to ask Dad what he thought she should do.

No one was in the kitchen or living room or backyard, and when she finally found Dad in his study he wasn't alone. As Neely approached the study door she began to hear voices. High, hard, angry voices, but muffled—like whispered screams. She couldn't make out everything they were saying, but she did hear Mom say, "John! He has to

face up to this, and so do you. For once in your life you
have to make yourself . . ."

There was more, but Neely didn't quite catch it because
Dad's voice cut in. What he was saying was harder to hear,
and then for a while they both seemed to be talking at once,
but one time when Dad's voice got louder she heard him
say, "You're absolutely wrong, Connie. You don't understand Grub at all. You never have." But then Neely accidentally bumped the door with her toe and there were
shushing sounds and then silence.

She was backing away on tiptoe when the voices started
up again, but more softly now. After that she could make
out even less of what they were actually talking about, but
she kept hearing some words over and over again. At first
the things they were saying seemed to be about Grub and
Robinson, but then some different words became a part of
it. Words like *Willie* and *Salinas* and later others like *blame*
and *fault*. At last she tiptoed down the hall and out onto the
front porch. Sitting down on the steps, she stared out at the
ocean.

For a while she only sat and stared and thought how just
last night she had sat at the very same spot and told herself
that the summer was starting out so well. . . . And now
. . . She sighed and let her head drop down until her forehead rested on her knees. Sitting there she began to feel a
swirling sensation as if the floor was dropping out from
under her. As if a strong floor that had always kept everything safe and comfortable had begun to dissolve and she
was about to go floating off into empty space. Empty space,
endless and dark and . . . Lifting her head, she opened

her eyes to see if there really was darkness—and saw instead a small red Honda turning off the highway onto Hutchinson Road.

"Lucie," she yelled, leaping to her feet. As she ran at top speed all the way down the steep, slippery driveway she went on calling, "Lucie, Lucie, Lucie." The red Honda stopped at the beginning of the drive and Lucinda Bradford, Neely's twenty-one-year-old sister, rolled down the window and said, "Neely, you nutcase. You're going to break your silly—" But then she really looked at Neely and said, "What is it? Neely, for God's sake, what's wrong?"

Neely staggered around the car and climbed into the passenger seat. "Oh, Lucie," she gasped when she could get enough breath to say anything. "Everything's wrong. Robinson's dead, and Grub's heart is broken, and Mom and Dad are having a terrible fight. Oh, Lucie, they're going to get a divorce. I just know they are."

Lucie reached out and pulled her close and for several minutes Neely sobbed and gasped and dripped a steady stream of tears onto Lucie's T-shirt. Lucie kept patting her back and saying, "Okay. Okay, Neely. It can't be that bad," and after a while Neely pulled away and used the bottom of her own T-shirt to sop up the rest of her tears.

Lucie smiled at her, a smile that sympathized but at the same time teased a little, like maybe saying, "Well, aren't we being wildly dramatic today?"—which was something Lucie used to say to Neely quite a lot. Lucie, who had always been a world-class teaser, would probably find something to tease about in the middle of a war or a killer earthquake. She gave Neely another quick hug and then reached out and turned off the ignition. "Well now," she said, "that's better. So tell me. From the very beginning."

CHAPTER
13

So NEELY TOLD LUCIE THE LONG, SAD STORY. ALL ABOUT Grub and Robinson and then about the terrible fight their parents were having in the study. When she finished, Lucie sighed and said, "Well, that's a real downer about poor old Robinson. *And* poor little Grubbie. But he'll get over it, you know. Everybody does. I had a cat that got it when I was about Grub's age. And Aaron had a dog. A really wonderful dog."

"I know," Neely said. "Stooge." Stooge had died before she was born, but she remembered hearing about him and seeing his picture in Aaron's picture album. "But Grub is . . . Grub's different."

"True," Lucie said. "Grub is one of a kind. The trouble with Grub is . . . he's absolutely skinless."

Neely wiped her eyes, sniffed, and frowned at Lucie. She didn't like other people making remarks about Grub. "What do you mean, skinless?"

"You know. You know how people say that if you get hurt too easily you're thin-skinned? Well, our Grubbie just hasn't any skin at all."

"Humph," Neely grunted. "Maybe so. But it's not just getting hurt more than other people, you know. He feels good things more too. Most of the time Grub is a lot happier than other people."

"I know," Lucie said. "And he will be again. Like I said, he'll get over Robinson. But now, about this thing with Mom and Dad."

"I know." Neely sighed. "They're going to get a divorce. I just know they are. They were saying awful things to each other."

Lucie grinned. "No, they aren't going to get a divorce, Neely baby. Dad and Mom are crazy about each other. They're just very different and that's why they love each other, but it's why they fight too. You've heard them fighting before, haven't you? And they haven't gotten a divorce yet."

"Well, little fights, maybe. But not like this one. Not nearly as bad as this one."

"Well, maybe not," Lucie said. "But I've certainly heard some bad ones before. In fact I think they used to fight more when Aaron and Julie and I were at home. Maybe we drove them to it. The three of us must have been a lot harder to live with than you and Grub. You've always been such a . . . well, such a solid-citizen type, and Grub . . . well, Grub is Grub."

Neely frowned. She didn't quite like the way Lucie said *solid citizen*, like it was something amusing, or maybe a little bit boring. But she'd think about that later. "What did they fight about then?" she asked. "When you were little?"

"Probably pretty much the same kinds of things they were fighting about today. You said you heard them saying something about *Willie* and *the Salinas property*? You know what that's about, don't you?"

"Well," Neely said. "Sort of." Willie probably referred to Dad's cousin, William Logan. She'd didn't know Willie very well because Mom didn't seem to like him very much. So even though Willie and his wife, Brenda, lived in the Salinas valley, which wasn't all that far away, there'd never been much visiting back and forth. "I know Mom doesn't like Willie very much because she thinks the land in the valley ought to belong to us instead of to him," Neely said.

"You got it," Lucie said. "But do you know why?"

"Not really."

"Well, what happened was that when Dad was away living in Berkeley, at the university at first and then with Mom after they were married, Willie came here and lived with Grandpa and helped out with the motel and the Salinas farm, and then after Grandpa died Willie claimed that he'd been promised the Salinas valley land. But the thing is, Grandpa's will didn't say so. The will left everything to Dad except for a few thousand dollars to Willie. So legally Dad could have kept the property. But he didn't because Willie didn't have zip, not a red cent, and Dad did inherit this place and the motel. And Willie *had* lived with Grandpa and helped him out for so long. But Mom thought we should have had the farm, too, and now that it's making a lot of money it really bugs her that Willie has it all.

Especially now with Aaron in medical school and me in college and you and Grub still to educate." Lucie shrugged and sighed and then she laughed. "The thing is, Mom loves Dad for being a softhearted old cream puff, but sometimes she hates him for it too."

Neely couldn't help grinning, too, even though she was still sniffing and sobbing a little. "I know," she said. "Like how mad she got when he tried to get her to be the one to fire Angie." Angie had been a maid at the motel who kept stealing lipsticks and eye shadow from the guests. "I mean, Dad just couldn't do it even after he'd caught Angie red-handed."

"Right," Lucie said. "Red-handed and red-lipped too. That's Dad all right. He's just too softhearted for his own good."

"Then you don't think they're going to get a divorce?" Neely asked.

"Nope. Never. Believe me, Neely. Connie and John Bradford are not getting a divorce. Not now, not ever." She got a Kleenex out of her purse and gave it to Neely, turned on the ignition, and drove on up the driveway to the house.

Watching Lucie gun the car up the steep graveled driveway and then maneuver skillfully into the narrow space between the garage and the oak tree, Neely suddenly felt a lot better. Lucie was so sure and certain about everything, maybe she was right about Mom and Dad too.

At dinner that night everything did seem pretty much okay. Lucie talked about her summer job at the university and her latest boyfriend, and Mom got out the new pictures of Julie and Ted's baby and talked about how sad it was that

Julie and Ted and her only grandchild lived so far away. Everyone talked a lot except Grub, but at least he was there at the table.

Grub had come out of his room just before dinner, and during the meal he even listened to Neely's plans for Robinson's funeral and said okay. He looked pretty much all right. The red was almost gone from his eyes and his eyelashes were dry and furry again. The rest of the family seemed to think he was entirely back to normal.

That night when Neely was getting into bed Lucie stuck her head in the door and said, "See, I was right, wasn't I? No divorce, and Grub's just fine."

And Neely said, "Sure, Lucie. You're always right. Everybody knows that." But actually she wasn't so sure. Oh, Lucie was probably right about Mom and Dad. After all, she had known them a lot longer than Neely had, and besides she'd taken all those college courses with titles like "Marriage and the Family," so she probably was pretty much of an expert on things like parents and divorce. But she wasn't an expert on Grub. Nobody in the world knew Grub as well as Neely did, and she was pretty certain that Grub wasn't anywhere near as okay as Lucie seemed to think he was.

CHAPTER
14

THEY HAD THE FUNERAL THE FIRST THING THE NEXT morning. Grub picked out a place for the grave between the chicken run and the rabbit hutch, and Dad helped him dig the hole. Lucie helped Neely decorate the cardboard coffin and Neely finished painting Robinson's picture on the tombstone she'd made from the central panel of an old chair back. Then the whole family made a procession around the property carrying the coffin and stopping in all the places Robinson had liked best—such as the arbor where he often slept on the sunny end of the picnic table and the vegetable garden where he liked to hunt for gophers. While they walked they sang *We Are the World*, which Grub said was Robinson's favorite song.

Grub seemed to handle it very well. He didn't cry, at least not out loud. Not even when Dad put the coffin down into the grave. When it was over everyone hugged him and said how brave he'd been and how proud they were of him.

Neely said it, too, but she didn't mean it. What she really was feeling was worried.

Something was definitely different about Grub. Something hushed and deadened. She saw it in his eyes and in the tight way he held his mouth when they were all hugging him. But there was no use mentioning it to the others since they obviously thought everything was okay. And Neely also knew there was no use trying to ask Grub about it because he probably didn't understand it himself.

Lucie stayed almost until dark on Sunday and she and Neely had another talk while they were weeding the garden. At first they talked about Grub, and Lucie sort of said "I told you so" about how quickly Grub was getting over Robinson. Neely didn't argue. And then, mostly to change the subject, she started talking about Willie and Dad and the valley property. "I guess there wouldn't have been any problem if Dad had come home after he finished college," she said. "Why *did* Dad stay in Berkeley instead of coming back to the coast?"

Lucie laughed. "Good question. You know how he's always raving about the 'old homestead' and how he was born with the wild and wonderful Big Sur coast in his blood. But he just wasn't cut out to be a Salinas valley vegetable farmer, and that's what Grandpa wanted him to be. What Dad really wanted to do was teach literature at the university. But then before he finished graduate school he married Mom and they bought the bookstore instead."

"Yeah," Neely said. "I know about that." She'd heard a lot about the bookstore from Mom and Dad, who seemed to remember it quite differently. Dad's bookstore memories seemed to be about meeting interesting customers and reading all the great books, and Mom remembered worries about money and paying taxes.

It wasn't until they'd pretty much covered the subject of the Bradfords in the pre–Neely-and-Grub days that Neely brought up the Hutchinsons and Halcyon House. The first thing she asked was if Lucie had ever met any of the Hutchinsons.

"Me?" Lucie said. "No, I never did. How old do you think I am, anyway? Dad remembers seeing all the cars going up to the mansion when he was a little boy, and then when he was a teenager I think he met Harold the third and his brother a few times. But even by then the family had stopped spending very much time on the coast. I think it was in the sixties, after Harold the second died, that they really stopped coming to Halcyon altogether. I don't know why exactly. Maybe they couldn't afford to come, or maybe they just weren't as crazy about the place anymore. What made you think about the Hutchinsons?"

"Oh, I don't know." Neely was a little disappointed that Lucie hadn't much information that was new and exciting. "I was just wondering."

It wasn't until Lucie left to go back to Santa Cruz that Neely had a chance to talk to Grub. She found him in his room sitting on the edge of his bed, not reading or playing with anything. Just sitting. When she stuck her head in the door and said, "Hi," he smiled and said, "Hi," back. But the smile wasn't real. He was in a mood, all right. A bad one.

Neely came in and sat down at the end of the bed.

"Look," she said. "I'm bored. How would you like to play a game of checkers? Or dominoes? Or maybe Scrabble?"

Grub looked all around before he answered, as if he hoped a good answer to Neely's question were written somewhere on the walls of the room. Then he shook his head and said, "No. I don't feel like playing a game. Not right now."

Neely began to feel frustrated. "Well, what do you feel like then, you little dweeb? Just sitting there moping all evening?"

"I'm not moping," Grub said. "I'm going to . . . I'm going to . . . read a book." He got up off the bed, went to his bookcase, and picked up a book—without even looking to see what it was. "See. I'm going to read this book." He held it out toward Neely and smiled.

There was something so pitiful about Grub's phony smile that Neely felt guilty for getting mad at him. "Okay," she said. "Read your book. But let's do something special tomorrow. Okay? Something fun."

"Okay." Grub nodded, but his eyes said he didn't much care one way or the other. "Like what?"

"Well . . ." Neely racked her brain, and came up with: "Hey, I know. Tomorrow's Monday. We could go to Halcyon House."

Grub looked up quickly. "And go inside?" he asked.

"No. Not inside. We can't *do* that anymore. It's too . . . dangerous."

"Oh." Grub shrugged and turned away.

"Well," Neely said. "I don't know. We could just go

there and see about it. We could visit Lion and *see* about going inside."

"Okay." A spark flickered in Grub's eyes. "Let's go see about it."

CHAPTER
15

BUT THEY DID GO INSIDE HALCYON HOUSE THE NEXT DAY because, as it turned out, nothing else worked. Nothing else—not playing with Lion or watching the tadpoles, even though they were beginning to grow hind legs and were pretty interesting, or making up a new game to play in the stable—did very much to change Grub's mood. It wasn't until Neely suggested that maybe they could go back inside the house again, *just for a little while*, that Grub began to pull out of it.

"Okay," he said, turning quickly to look at Neely. "We'll just stay for a little while."

"Right!" Neely said as they climbed up the wisteria vine and made their way carefully across the slippery shingles. "Just for a little while—and for the last time. That's for sure."

Opening the window was a little easier, but it still required quite a bit of tugging and pulling, and while Neely was still working at it Grub squeezed through ahead of her. She was just starting through herself, on her stomach, when from inside the room she heard Grub saying loudly, "We're only going to stay a little while today." But by the time she'd scrambled to her feet he was going through the drawers of the dressing table, and when she asked who he'd been talking to he only shrugged and smiled and said, "Myself. I was just talking to myself."

They started at the top floor ballroom that day and really didn't stay very long, at least not up there. Just long enough for Grub to play one record and for Neely to walk quickly around the long room, stopping briefly to look out the window behind the bandstand. The one with the window seat in front of the great view down into the canyon and then on out to the ocean.

On the other floors, too, they moved fairly quickly. As they entered each room Grub ran around opening drawers and cupboards and making comments about what was inside. He found old clothes and papers mostly, but sometimes interesting things like a hairbrush and mirror set with tarnished silver backs, a beautiful crystal paper weight shaped like a rose, and a collection of fancy perfume bottles.

Sometimes Neely went to look at what Grub had found, but mostly she just stood still, looking and listening. Looking to see if Grub was leaving any noticeable foot- or fingerprints in the dust and listening for whatever it was she couldn't quite hear. After a few minutes of uneasy listening and watching she whispered, "Stop that, Grub. Stop touching things. And come on. We have to hurry." Then she went around quickly smudging out Grub's foot- and finger-prints before they left the room.

So their visit might really have been a short one if it hadn't been for what happened in the library. After stopping briefly to stare at the family portrait over the fireplace, Neely began to read the titles on the old books. Most of them seemed to be about history or travel, but in a small alcove she came across some old children's books. She sat down on the padded bench that was built into the back of the alcove, and for a little while forgot about hurrying.

Most of the books were about animals, mostly horses and dogs. And the ones that weren't about animals seemed to be about girls. There was *Little Women, Rebecca of Sunnybrook Farm, The Secret Garden*, and some others she'd not heard of before. But all obviously about girls. Still holding an armload of books, Neely went back to look again at the portrait and particularly at the little girl with the big eyes and the faint sad smile. Then she went back to sit on the padded bench again.

There was a peacefulness there in the alcove, and a different kind of quietness. A hush that didn't feel like a barrier behind which other sounds were hiding. The silence in the library felt deep and real. The alcove was, she decided, the kind of place where someone could come and curl up with a book and feel private and secret and safe.

Neely had looked at several books and was a page or two into a horse story called *Black Beauty* when she heard a jingle and Grub stuck a bunch of keys under her nose. Heavy old bronze keys with large oval-shaped heads, each with a decorative border surrounding an engraved number.

"Look, Neely," he said. "Keys. There's eleven of them. I found them in that big old desk down there by the windows. Let's go see if one of them is for the locked room."

As Neely stared at the keys she felt it again, the sudden deep beat of fear that came from somewhere near the pit of her stomach. She shook her head quickly. "No. No, we couldn't do that." But even while she was saying it she could feel another part of her mind beginning to wonder. To wonder if one of the keys would really unlock the door, and if it did . . . what might be inside. "Grub," she said. "We can't do that. We haven't any right to open that door. And besides, the right key probably isn't there."

Grub looked at the keys. "I know. It probably isn't. But we could try them. You know, as a kind of experiment."

Neely took the keys from him. They weren't like any keys she'd ever seen before. They felt odd in her hand— heavy and brassy. "Well," she said. "I guess we could just try. But it probably isn't one of these."

She was still telling herself that the key to the locked room certainly wouldn't be right there on the ring with all the others when they got to the door.

"Look," Grub said. "They match." He pointed to the keys and then to the bronze plate that surrounded the doorknob and keyhole. The embossed border pattern on the keyplate was the same as on the keys themselves.

"I know." Neely nodded. "But that doesn't mean anything. All the doors have keyplates like that. That doesn't mean one of these keys will open this door. The key to this door is probably locked away somewhere in a safe, or a secret drawer."

Grub nodded. "Probably in a secret drawer," he said. "In books they always find keys to mysterious places in secret drawers, don't they?"

Neely tried the keys in order, the number one first and then the one labeled two. When she got to number eight she stopped to say, "I told you so," but then the very next key made a rusty clicking sound and turned—all the way around inside the lock. Grub reached out quickly and turned the knob.

The door opened on dark shadows and the smell of dust and mildew. Against dim light that filtered in through heavy drapes, dust hung in the air and swirled in small eddies where it had been stirred by the opening door. Neely coughed and covered her mouth and nose with her hand.

"I'm going to open the drapes," Grub said. She grabbed his arm to hold him back, but he pulled away and began to make his way toward the windows, around large vague shapes that seemed to loom up in his path. Neely started after him and whacked her shin on something that made a creaking sound and began to move. She reached out quickly to keep it from falling and her hand touched something that felt like coarse hair. She jumped back, squealing with fright, but just at that moment Grub reached the windows and pulled back the drapes.

Blinking in the sudden light, Neely gradually became aware of a large room cluttered with boxes and chests and several pieces of furniture. Small, child-size furniture. And toys! Toys were everywhere, scattered across the floor, piled up in the corners, and crowding the shelves that ran around two sides of the room. Old-fashioned toys, the kind you sometimes saw in the windows of antique stores—old style cars, trucks, and trains, model forts full of toy soldiers, and model farmyards full of wooden horses, cows, and chickens. Against one wall there was a huge three-story doll house, and near the door stood a large rocking horse with a horse-hair mane—the strange hairy creature that Neely had stumbled against in the dark.

And everywhere, coating every object and swirling in the disturbed air, there was dust. The thick, heavy, ancient dust of long, lonely years.

CHAPTER
16

GRUB CAUGHT HIS BREATH IN A LONG DRAWN OUT "ohhh," and then sneezed twice.

"It's the dust," Neely said. She poked him. "See, I told you so. It's just a dusty old nursery. Nothing mysterious at all—and no bones."

Grub nodded and started gasping. In between gasps he managed to say, "I never said . . . there'd be . . . bones," before he sneezed again and went on sneezing. When he finally stopped he sniffed, wiped his eyes, and gave Neely one of his supergorgeous smiles. "Let's dust it, Neely," he said.

"Dust it?" Neely was astonished. It was a thought that for some reason caused a crawling sensation up the back of her neck. To clean a floor where no human foot had stepped for many long lonely years and to dust—she stopped to look around—to dust a toy soldier that no hands had held since . . .

Her shoulders twitched in a sharp shiver. A shiver that seemed a little bit about fear—but mostly about a bunch of excited questions that were spinning through her mind. Questions about whose hands had last held the toy, and what the owners of the hands would think if they knew that she and Grub were there in their room. And if it were possible that they did know. . . .

She shook her head sharply, and came back to Grub's suggestion—and to the surprising thought that there really wasn't any reason why they shouldn't clean the room a little if they wanted to. It wasn't as if Reuben might discover what they'd done when he came in to clean, because he obviously never did. Not in this room anyway. It was very obvious that no one had been in this room for many, many years.

What she was careful not to think about was why they should *want* to clean a room they weren't going to be in for much longer—and after today not ever again.

"I know where there's a bunch of cleaning stuff," Grub said. "In the closet next to that butler's pantry. There's a broom and a feather duster and a dustpan and all kinds of stuff."

Neely looked around the room again, at the enormous dollhouse against the far wall, at the toys piled and crowded together on the shelves—old-fashioned windup toys made of tin—and at the enormous stuffed animals: a bear, a rabbit, a tiger. Then smaller animals made of all sorts of other materials: glass swans and unicorns, china pigs and dogs, and other animals made of everything from plaster to what seemed to be tarnished silver. There were also the soldiers: armies of tiny soldiers in old-fashioned uniforms carrying swords and muskets and flags. And on the top shelf what looked like enough equipment for a small orchestra: drums and horns and tambourines and even a violin and a small-size accordion.

"Okay," she said. "Come on." And taking hold of Grub's arm she headed for the door and the closet next to the butler's pantry.

They began by opening the windows. Neely would have liked to take down the heavy drapes, but since they had no ladder they settled for brushing them down with the broom. There were lots of spiderwebs and the dust was awful. They both sneezed continuously until Neely thought of making dust masks by pulling the necks of their T-shirts up to just below their eyes like the veils worn by Arabian women.

After the drapes they did the shelves. They dusted the soldiers with the feather duster, shook the stuffed animals out the window, and polished the toy musical instruments. Their progress was slowed by the temptation to stop and play, or at least to explore the possibilities—like how many of the windup toys still worked and what sorts of sounds could be made with the musical instruments. The furniture came next and then the floor, a slow job complicated by a clutter of train tracks, forts, and barnyards.

Much to Neely's surprise Grub worked fast and efficiently. Not that he was usually opposed to work. He always started any chore Mom gave him to do without much complaining. It was just that he tended to lose track of what he was doing and wander off in a daydream long before the job was finished. But cleaning up the old nursery seemed to hold his attention better than ordinary work. And as he swept and dusted, from behind his T-shirt mask there came the familiar sound of humming.

In fact it was Neely who had a hard time keeping her mind on what she was doing. While Grub hummed and dusted without pausing, she found herself stopping now and then—bent over the broom, or with one hand lifted to dust—not to daydream but to listen and imagine. To listen for the voices and laughter that had once echoed from the faded wallpapered walls, and to imagine the slightest echo of warmth left by the fingers that long ago held the silver elephant that now lay in the palm of her hand.

It wasn't until she began cleaning the dollhouse that she forgot to watch and listen. She'd saved it till last because it was so wonderful. Unfortunately it was completely empty, but even with no furniture or people it was fascinating—its many rooms were beautifully finished with tiny plaster fireplaces, windows of real glass, painted rugs, and a grand curving stairway leading from floor to floor. She was working on the living room, clearing out the cobwebs and dusting the floor, when Grub called to her.

"Neely." He sounded excited. "Come here. See what I found."

When Neely came out from behind the dollhouse she saw that Grub was kneeling in front of a large trunk. She had noticed it before when she'd been sweeping the corner of the room where it sat against the wall. She particularly noticed its large size, the dome-shaped lid of stamped metal reinforced with bent wood slats, and the fact that it seemed to be full of something heavy. She had also checked carefully and found that it was *locked*. But now the domed lid was wide open.

CHAPTER
17

As neely started across the room she said, "hey, what are you doing? That trunk was locked, Grub."

Grub's blue eyes in their frame of fuzzy lashes were wide and innocent. "I know," he said. "But I just jiggled it a little. See, like this . . . and it went click and came open."

"Jiggled it? What do you mean you . . ." Neely began and then fizzled out as she stared down into the trunk. The top level of the trunk was a deep tray and it was full of the most beautiful dollhouse furniture she had ever seen. Tables, chairs, beds, dressers, lamps, and cabinets all carefully and intricately fashioned of shiny dark hardwood. There were upholstered chairs, beds complete with tiny quilts and blankets, and cabinets with doors that really opened and held sets of dishes and silverware. Neely was still opening tiny drawers and cupboards when Grub lifted one end of the tray by its leather handle and peeked under. "There's a doll down there," he said. "A big one."

There was a doll, an old china-headed doll with stiff brown curls, a body of soft leather, and eyes that opened and shut. She was dressed in a blue-and-white plaid dress with a middy blouse collar and her black shoes were shiny patent leather.

The rest of the trunk held other toys. Lots and lots of horses, for one thing. Horses of all shapes and sizes, made of everything from plaster to tarnished silver.

And then there were dolls. Boy and girl and baby dolls, and a great deal of doll clothing of various sizes. In a separate box there were a number of little dolls that had obviously been the occupants of the beautiful dollhouse—an entire family including children and servants. Tiny dolls, with jointed arms and legs, elegantly dressed in old-fashioned clothing—the women in long dresses, the little boy in short pants, and the girl in a ruffled pinafore.

Beneath the layer of dolls there were sets of doll dishes, and at the bottom, under several large envelopes full of elaborate old-fashioned paper dolls, there was a half-finished sampler still stretched on a wooden embroidery frame.

The top half of the sampler consisted of a picture of a house, a tree, and a girl in a sunbonnet. Below the picture was an alphabet and around the outer edge there was a border of vines and flowers. The house and the tree were finished in tiny cross-stitch in many bright colors and each of the letters of the alphabet was done in a different shade. There were reds, blues, greens, yellows, and then a half-finished lavender letter *K*. The embroidered work ended there.

Just below the *K* a needle was still pinned into the cloth —a needle still threaded with lavender embroidery cotton. The colors of the embroidery thread were still bright and clear but the inked pattern on the unfinished part of the sampler had faded almost away. The printed letters from *L* to *Z* were barely legible.

"Look." Grub was pointing to some very faint lettering at the bottom of the sampler. "It says something else after the alphabet. Something that starts with an *M*."

"Yes, it's an *M*," Neely said. "And maybe an *A* next, but the rest of it is all faded. But on the other side it's clearer. See, it looks like it was supposed to say *Age 10*."

Grub picked up the sampler and stared at it for a long time. "That was when she disappeared," he said, "when she was ten. While she was working on the *K*." He looked around the room. "And then they took all her things and put them in this trunk. Because the others were afraid to touch her things ever again."

"Or because there weren't any other girls in the family," Neely said. "They probably just stored away all the girl toys because there weren't any other girls in the family to play with them."

"Umm." Grub nodded, but then he pointed to the horses and said, "How about those? Boys could play with horses." He nodded some more before he said, "I think they were afraid."

But when Neely asked him what they were afraid of he only shook his head. "I don't know," he said. "Don't you know, Neely?"

She didn't know, of course, and she really didn't believe

it. Right at that moment it made her a little nervous even to think about why people might have been afraid to touch the toys in the old chest.

For several minutes after Grub went away to play with the toy train she sat on the floor in front of the giant chest trying not to think about why all the girl-type toys were locked away. It wasn't until she picked up the first piece of furniture—a beautiful lady's dressing table—carried it to the dollhouse, and found just the right spot for it in one of the bedrooms, that she began to forget about being nervous.

CHAPTER
18

IT WAS QUITE LATE WHEN NEELY AND GRUB GOT HOME
that day. They were still washing their faces in the laundry
tub on the back porch when the kitchen door opened and
Mom came out. She was clutching a wooden spoon and
smelled of marmalade.

"There you are," she said. "Where have you been? I
was beginning to worry."

"But we told you we were going to the grove," Neely
said. "We always stay a while when we go there."

"A while yes, but this was"—Mom looked at her watch
—"more like four hours. And look at yourselves. You're
filthy. What on earth were you doing?"

Grub tried to brush off his T-shirt. "Not filthy," he
said. "Just dusty."

"Dusty?" Mom asked. "What were you doing that was
so dusty?"

Neely bit her lip, but she needn't have worried. Grub only said, "We were just playing. It was a very dusty game."

"It must have been," Mom said. "Just look at your clothes. You weren't digging in the grove, were you? You know that's private land and you actually haven't any right to be there at all. And you certainly haven't the right to—" She stopped, sniffed, and said, "Oh, dear, my marmalade."

While Mom rushed back to the stove to rescue the marmalade, Neely and Grub managed to escape to their rooms. By the time they emerged, cleaned and changed, Mom was too busy sealing the jars of marmalade with hot paraffin to worry about a little dust.

During the next few days Neely thought a lot about the nursery and the girl whose name had apparently started with an *M*. Thought—and dreamed. Sitting on the front steps, or in the window seat, or curled up on her bed, Neely became "*M.*" Instead of Beth March or Joan of Arc or the little mermaid, or any of her other recent favorites, she became the pretty girl in the portrait at Halcyon House. A rich girl who lived in fabulous yachts and palaces all over the world, visited all kinds of exciting places like the pyramids and the Tower of London, and then came back every summer to stay at Halcyon. Came back to sleep in the room with the sleigh-shaped bed—and play in the nursery with the beautiful dollhouse and the other fantastic old toys.

And probably, since it certainly seemed that she had loved horses, to keep her own horse in the Halcyon House stable. A snow-white Arabian mare, Neely decided. And to ride alone up into the mountains or down to the coast where she would race the waves along the beach. That was the scene Neely came back to most often—galloping through the ocean foam with her long blond hair mingling with the flowing white mane of her own Arabian mare.

Usually she ended the story there, but sometimes it went on to the tragic ending. On to the unfinished sampler and to what happened after the lavender *K*. To why the work on the sampler had ended and it was stored away, along with all her other toys, in the trunk with the domed lid.

In Neely's imaginings the tragic ending of the story was never quite the same. Sometimes, as she had told Grub, it was a sudden disappearance, but other times it was a terrible disease. A mysterious disease like the ones people died from in old books, like consumption, or wasting, or simply from a broken heart. Before and after and in between the daydreams Neely also spent quite a lot of time trying to remember exactly what it was she had heard Greta say about the Hutchinson girl who died young—but it had been a long time ago and the memory was blurry.

The more she thought about it the less sure she became just how much she'd really overheard. She wasn't sure, for instance, how much of what she'd told Grub, there on the bench in the rose garden, had been what Greta actually said, and how much had just been one of the "new parts" that Grub liked to have added to stories.

But Grub seemed to believe it was true. At least he seemed to be quite certain that something very strange and mysterious had happened to the little girl who died at Halcyon. And that explained why he thought there was some weird reason that those particular toys were locked away in the dome-topped trunk.

Neely wished she knew exactly what Grub believed, but of course she wouldn't ask him. To ask Grub if he really believed something would be to break the *rule*. The *rule* that, in the past for instance, had kept Grub from asking her if she'd really seen a unicorn in Halcyon Grove, and had kept her from asking him if he'd really seen a pirate ship anchored off Point Lobos. To start asking that kind of question would be to ruin everything.

CHAPTER
19

OF COURSE, THERE WAS ONE WAY NEELY COULD FIND OUT some of what she needed to know. She could ask Greta Peale herself. However, that wouldn't be particularly easy. For one thing, it couldn't be done on the telephone because Greta was too deaf. That left going to see her, which presented a different problem: Neely needed to talk to Greta without Grub being there, and Grub loved visiting old Miss Peale. But then Mom mentioned that Grub had a dentist appointment on Wednesday afternoon and Neely's plan began to take shape.

As soon as Mom and Grub left for the dentist's, Neely started in on Dad about how Miss Peale was overdue for a Bradford family visit and some vegetables from Mom's garden. The Peales, like the Bradfords, had been old pioneer families, and the Peale property was only about two miles down the coast. Miss Peale, who was almost ninety years old, had lived there all her life and had known Dad since he was born. According to Dad Greta Peale had once been one of the pioneer women of the Big Sur coast—one of the wild, strong, beautiful women that the poets and storytellers had written about. But now she was old and frail and walked with a cane. When Dad said he was too busy with the motel's payroll book to go visiting, Neely reminded him of something he'd told her himself.

"Remember how Greta used to bring you and Mom vegetables and fruit when you first moved back here from Berkeley and you had Aaron and Julie and Lucie and not much money and Mom was pregnant with me?"

Dad smiled. "I certainly do," he said, "but I doubt if you do."

"Of course I don't actually remember it," Neely said. "But I've heard about it lots of times. And now she's old and lonely and too crippled to grow her own garden anymore."

"I give up," Dad said. "Go pick some tomatoes and lots of zucchinis. Greta loves zucchinis."

When Dad and Neely drove up in front of the old Peale farmhouse in Dad's pickup truck Greta was sitting on her front porch. She was wearing a bright colored shawl over a flowing black dress and her heavy white hair was wrapped around her head in a thick braid. Her weathered face was wrinkled into deep cracks and crevices and burned by the sun to almost the same color as the craggy cliffs of her beloved coast, but her eyes were still as wild and blue as the Pacific Ocean.

"Beautiful zucchinis," she said as she led the way into

the house. "Picked at just the right time. Most people let them grow too big."

"I picked them," Neely said. "I remembered you like little ones."

"Did you?" Greta stopped, and putting one hand under Neely's chin, she turned her toward the light. She studied Neely's face for a long time before she said, "Strength. A good strong face. Not a Bradford face"—she looked at Dad and smiled teasingly—"with all that unprotected pain and joy, but a lovely face full of confidence and grace."

Then she let go of Neely's chin and gestured toward the living room. "Now you two just go right on in and sit down. I'll be with you as soon as I put these gorgeous things away."

Neely and Dad grinned at each other and Dad said, "Right. Come on, Miss Confidence and Grace. And Determination too. The third name is Determination." Then he patted Neely's shoulder and led the way into the cluttered living room where he sat down on the saggy old couch while Neely wandered around looking at ancient keepsakes and dim photographs of old pioneer families. When Greta came in with wine and cider and cookies, the talk began.

As usual at Greta's, most of the talk was about the old times before the highway went in when the Big Sur coast was wild and free. Dad didn't really remember those days but he'd grown up hearing about them, and since his parents had been real coast pioneers Greta considered him one too. They talked about old Doc Roberts, and the Pfeiffers, the Sharpes and Douds, and the Posts, and of course about the famous poet, Robinson Jeffers. Neely sat and listened for a long time before she brought up the subject of the Hutchinsons.

Greta shrugged. "Summer people," she said. "Rich summer people." Her tone of voice said they weren't really worth mentioning, but fortunately she did go on talking. "I remember hearing my father say that old Harold the first, the one who built Halcyon, got his money in some pretty shady ways. And there were rumors of worse than that. Blackmail, and maybe even murder. One of his competitors died under pretty suspicious circumstances. But then in his old age he supposedly saw the error of his ways and tried to repent. My father used to say old Harold came here and built Halcyon hoping that the peace and beauty of the Carmel coast would help him escape his evil past."

Greta stopped to pour herself another glass of wine. When she'd finished pouring Neely prompted, "Did he find any peace and beauty at Halcyon?"

Greta chuckled grimly. "The beauty is here for anyone with eyes to see it," she said, "but from all accounts any sort of peace and tranquility pretty much escaped poor old Harold. Got what he deserved, I'm afraid. Over the years there were all kinds of accidents and sickness, along with things like alcoholism and insanity. Not to mention a lot of pretty bitter family feuds."

"They were star-crossed," Neely said. "I heard you telling Mom that the Hutchinsons were star-crossed." And then, hurriedly, while Greta was still in a reminiscing mood, "And wasn't there a little girl who died when she was only ten? I heard you telling Mom about that once. Did you know her, that little girl who died?"

"Not really," Greta said. "The Hutchinsons didn't mix much with real coast people. But I was asked to a party once. A birthday party for Monica when she was eight years old and I was just a year or so older. There never were many girls in the Hutchinson family and I suppose they thought she needed at least one little girl guest for that particular event and I happened to be the handiest one." She paused, staring with blank, unfocused eyes, as if into a faraway distance. "Only time I ever saw Monica," she said, "or that fantastic house. Never will forget that fantastic house."

"Monica." Remembering the *M* on the sampler, Neely tried to keep from sounding too excited. "Was that her name?"

"Umm." Greta nodded thoughtfully. "Pretty little thing she was. Pity about her dying so young."

"What did she die of?" Neely asked.

Greta frowned and scratched her chin. After a while she said, "Pneumonia, I think. I think that's what the paper said it was."

Neely felt disappointed. She hadn't really believed the mysterious disappearance thing, but somehow she'd been expecting something at least a little strange and eerie. Or frightening. Something that might have frightened people —like Grub had said.

But then Greta went on. "There were rumors though."

"What kind of rumors?" Neely asked quickly.

"Oh, don't know if I can say for sure. It was so long ago. Something about how they didn't call Doc Roberts or anybody from around Monterey. Just called in some relative, and some folks said he wasn't even a proper doctor."

Greta Peale stopped to think, settling her glasses more firmly on her nose and pushing back a wisp of white hair. Then she nodded again and said, "Something strange about the whole thing. Caused a bit of gossip as I recall."

"Gossip?" Neely prompted eagerly.

Too eagerly maybe, because Greta looked at her with a questioning smile. "What an inquisitive child you are," she said, and then turning to Dad, "It's her coast blood, no doubt. We always were a nosy bunch out here, weren't we? Guess it's because there wouldn't have been much else to talk about way out here at the edge of the earth, if we hadn't gossiped about each other."

Dad laughed, but then he got up and said he had to get back to his books. "Come along, Neely," he said, "before you wear Greta out with your questions."

Neely followed reluctantly. Reluctant, but thrilled too. She couldn't wait to get home and tell Grub that the unfinished sampler, and everything in the old trunk, had belonged to a little girl named Monica.

CHAPTER
20

OF COURSE THEY WENT BACK TO HALCYON HOUSE. AFTER they'd discovered the nursery, the temptation was just too great. Even imagining being caught by Reuben and being dragged off to the police station wasn't enough to make Neely renew her promise never to do it again—not promise and actually mean it anyway. And as Grub said, "After all that work we can't just let it get dusty again. Can we, Neely?"

"I guess we can't," Neely told him. "It just wouldn't be right."

So they kept on going to Halcyon House. For the next two weeks they managed to visit the nursery on Monday mornings and Saturday afternoons, but only for a couple of hours so Mom wouldn't get suspicious. But in July everything changed. The change was because Sam and Betty Martin went to Massachusetts to be with Betty's mother who was very sick, so Mom and Dad had to take over as full-time managers at the motel.

For a while it looked like it was going to be every day at the motel for Grub and Neely too. And it might have been except that Neely did some fancy talking and persuaded Mom that she and Grub were old enough to stay home alone, at least now and then. "Not every day," she argued. "Just now and then. So Grub won't get so bored sitting around in that old motel office."

"Well, Grub doesn't have to sit in the office all day," Mom said. "Most boys his age would love to have a chance to spend some time in town. He could get out and see people like you do."

Sure he could, Neely thought, but he won't. Just because Mom thought that Grub ought to act more like other kids his age didn't mean that he would—or could. And his mom ought to know it. But Neely didn't say that. Instead she just kept on arguing that every day was too much time to spend in town, for her as well as for Grub. So Mom finally agreed to the two of them staying home alone "now and then." And of course the "now and then" turned out to be on Mondays and Saturdays.

So July was theirs. On the other days of the week they went into Carmel with Mom and Dad, but every Monday and Saturday they went to the grove early, taking along bag lunches. They hid in the fern patch until they saw Reuben go by and then ran all the way to the house, with Lion running joyfully beside them—to then sit and watch mournfully as they climbed to the veranda roof and disappeared from view. Once inside the house they hurried to the library for the key and then went directly to the nursery, to spend most of the day.

Monica spent most of her time with the dollhouse. Neely, of course, actually, but an early development in her game was that she became Monica as soon as she reached the nursery. She didn't know why exactly, except that she'd always pretended to be other people, usually people from her favorite books or movies. But there was more to being Monica than that. A part of it was that she simply felt more at ease that way. At ease, maybe, because while it seemed perfectly all right for ten-year-old Monica to play with a dollhouse, a sixth-grade middle school student was, perhaps, a little too old.

But there was another, much more important reason, and that was because she felt less guilty that way. Less guilty because Monica had a right to the magnificent dollhouse while Neely had none at all.

So it was as Monica that Neely arranged the beautiful pieces of furniture in the many rooms, and put away all the miniature dishes and pots and pans in their proper places. And as Monica she moved the doll family from room to room—sometimes scattering them through the house to sleep, play, or work in the various rooms. The nursemaid and the children in the nursery; the cook in the kitchen; the elegantly dressed adults in the luxurious living room, seated in front of the fireplace with its realistic-looking plaster fire.

While Neely thought up sophisticated conversations for the parent dolls, and invented interestingly tragic life histories for the sad-looking little nursemaid and the plump, red-cheeked cook, Grub played his own games. Once in a while he would come over to ask what was happening in the dollhouse, but most of the time he played by himself—with the farmyard animals, or the miniature circus, or the toy soldiers. And once in a while Neely checked to see what he was doing.

Usually when she peeked over the roof or through the windows of the dollhouse Grub would be sitting in the midst of a careful arrangement of animals or soldiers, moving them from place to place—and talking. Always talking softly, making the animals or soldiers talk to one another, or at least that was what Neely thought at first—until she noticed something strange.

The strange thing was that when Grub talked he usually wasn't looking down at the toy he was holding in his hand. Instead he seemed to be talking to someone or something that was sitting directly in front of him. Holding up a cow as if to show it to someone, or a cannon to demonstrate how it could be aimed up or down. It wasn't until she'd watched him do it several times that she decided to ask him about it.

Getting up from behind the dollhouse, she went over to where Grub was sitting cross-legged in front of the three wooden rings full of circus animals—a lion and tiger arrangement in one ring, a horse act with monkey riders in another, and a couple of clowns in the third.

"Hi," Grub said, looking up at Neely with one of his quick, shiny smiles. "We're playing circus."

Neely felt her heart give an extra beat. "So I see," she

said, and then after taking a quick breath, "We? What do you mean by we? You and who else?"

Grub looked surprised and then a little embarrassed. His eyes slid in the opposite direction and then came back. Then he looked down at the tiger in his hand. Turning it from side to side he almost whispered, "Monica. I was playing with Monica."

Neely found herself looking again—more carefully this time—at the place on the other side of the circus rings, directly across from where Grub was sitting, but of course there was nothing there. When she looked back at Grub he was still wide-eyed and smiling.

Neely swallowed hard. Gulping down the question that wanted to come out, she asked only, "Monica?"

"Umm." Grub nodded and started making the tiger jump back and forth through a hoop.

Neely went back to the dollhouse then, but she found it hard to get back into what she'd been doing. Instead she kept watching Grub—and particularly watching the empty space on the other side of the circus game. But no matter how hard she stared, or how quickly she turned to look at it again, the space went on being empty. And Grub went on nodding and smiling and talking to something—or someone—she couldn't see.

Once when Grub seemed to be having a particularly lively conversation she got to her feet and crossed the room to the far corner and the Monica trunk. Quietly lifting the lid and the tray she pawed through the doll clothes and dishes until she found it—the unfinished sampler. Then with the sampler between her hands she closed her eyes and thought first about the faded words at the bottom of the sampler picture—*Monica, Age 10.*—and then about the girl in the portrait over the library mantel. Then, as vividly as she could, she pictured the same little girl sitting on the floor next to Grub's circus game.

She waited until she could see Monica as plain as day. A pretty little girl, sitting there cross-legged, her curly blond head bent forward to see what Grub was doing. And then Neely opened her eyes. She opened them quickly and—for just a flicker of a second, while her eyes were still half opened—Monica was there. She was there—and then she was gone.

Neely put the sampler back in the trunk and hurried over to where Grub was sitting. "Come on, Grub," she said. "Let's go home. We have to go home right now."

Grub didn't argue.

CHAPTER
21

AFTER NEELY HAD TIME TO THINK IT OVER CAREFULLY SHE decided there was no reason to worry about Grub's "playing with Monica" game. Because it was, of course, only a game. Just as she, Neely, imagined being Monica when she was in the nursery, Grub was imagining that Monica was there with him, talking to him and playing his games. And what she'd seen, or thought she'd seen, sitting there across from Grub, had probably been only her imagination.

She was sure that was all there was to it, or almost sure, but once or twice she did ask Grub some questions. Not the "Is it true . . . ?" kind of question, of course, but just an occasional casual one like, "What kind of games does Monica like best?" or "What was Monica wearing today?"

Grub didn't seem to mind. When Neely asked that kind of question he always looked pleased, thought a moment and then said, "She likes playing with the circus best," or "Blue. She was wearing a blue dress with lace, like in the

picture in the library." And that was all. But that was perfectly all right, Neely decided. After all, what other kind of
an answer did she want?

It was toward the end of July that Reuben started water-
ing the lawn at Halcyon House. Not all of the acres of
weed-choked lawn in front of the house and down the hill
on one side, but just the small round section directly in
front of the entryway. Neely noticed it first on a Monday
and by the next Saturday the grass in the circle around the
fountain had become even greener and had recently been
mowed. It was on that same day that Grub pointed out that
the dead tree in the living room had been taken away and
all of its fallen leaves had been swept up.

On their next visit there were other signs that Reuben
was taking his job of caretaker more seriously. Other
rooms, both upstairs and down, were swept and dusted and
some of the dustcovers that protected the upholstered furniture had been taken away.

Neely was worried and it seemed to her that, even
though he didn't say so, Grub was worried too.

"Maybe we should stop coming," Neely said on the
Monday that they first noticed the missing dustcovers. "At
least for a little while," she added hastily when she saw the
look on Grub's face.

Grub shook his head violently. "No," he said. "It's
okay. I think Reuben is just doing spring cleaning."

"In July?" Neely said, smiling.

"Well, maybe he'd rather do summer cleaning, or
something," Grub said. "And besides, he won't go in the

nursery. He never did before. You said he never did before. Come on. Let's get the key."

On the last Saturday in July Neely was particularly anxious to get to the nursery because she'd thought of a new adventure for her dollhouse family to have. It had to do with some kidnappers who were going to try to steal the doll family's baby and hold it for ransom. She decided she'd have to use some of Grub's toy soldiers to be the kidnappers even though they were a little too small—and when she asked Grub if he wanted to be a part of the game he seemed very interested.

"I'll get the key," Grub said as soon as they crawled in the window. "I'll get it. You wait up here." Then he hurried off downstairs while Neely waited outside the nursery door, thinking about the kidnap game and deciding which member of the family would be the hero who saved the baby. When Grub came back with the key he was frowning.

"There's a new cupboard in the game room," he said as he handed Neely the key.

"A new cupboard?"

"Umm. A big one. With glass doors and guns inside. Four of them. There are four guns and two of them look like those army things."

"Really," Neely said. "Let's go see."

Grub was right. Sitting against the wall beyond the fireplace there was a large cabinet that definitely hadn't been there before. It was made of dark heavy wood and its padlocked door seemed to be made of the thick unbreakable glass you sometimes see around cashiers' booths. Inside you could see four guns hanging on racks against a velvet-covered back wall. Four very deadly-looking guns, two long ones and two short. Staring at the guns, Neely had a very uncomfortable feeling.

Grub looked worried too. "Neely?" he said, and it was definitely a question. Grub was asking her to explain the gun cabinet. To explain it—and to make it all right.

Neely bit her lip. "It—it must be Reuben's," she told Grub. "He'd probably have to have guns around, since his job is being a watchman. Watchmen usually have dogs and guns too. And you know how small his house is. He probably just decided to keep his gun cabinet in here. Look how big it is. It must have taken up half his living room in that little place."

Grub looked relieved. "Oh," he said, smiling happily. "It's just Reuben's watchman guns. That's okay then. Let's go play about the kidnappers."

He hurried off and Neely followed more slowly thinking about what she had told Grub—and hoping she was right. Hoping and worrying. But once she was back in the nursery and they'd started the kidnappers game she forgot about the gun cabinet, at least for a while.

It was probably about a half hour later, when Grub was making a toy soldier tiptoe around the outside of the dollhouse looking in all the windows, that he suddenly put the soldier down and turned to stare at the nursery door.

"Shhh!" he said.

Neely caught her breath. "What is it?" she whispered. "What is it? Did you hear something?"

"Sort of," Grub said. When he turned to look at Neely

his face looked tight and stiff and his eyes were huge. "Come on, Neely. We'd better go."

Then she heard it, too, a faint scuffling sound that seemed very close—like just outside the nursery door.

She was just getting to her feet when the doorknob turned, and the door opened a tiny crack. Something moved outside the crack and then stopped moving. Neely got to her feet and was starting around the dollhouse when a strange, high-pitched voice said, "Who—who are you?"

CHAPTER
22

FOR WHAT WAS PROBABLY ONLY A FEW SECONDS, BUT seemed like forever, nothing moved and no one spoke. Hanging on to the back of Grub's shirt, Neely stared at the door, too shocked even to think. The opening didn't widen and nothing could be seen through the narrow crack. But finally, after that silent eternity, the high, wobbly voice came again. "I *said*, who are you?" This time it definitely sounded young, like a girl perhaps, or a boy whose voice hadn't yet changed.

Neely swallowed hard, tried to speak, tried again and managed, "I'm Neely Bradford. Neely, and"—she gestured —"and Grub. Who—who are you?" There was no answer, but after a moment the door began to inch open. A head came through first. A lot of stiff, pale hair, and a round, lumpy face with pale, jittery eyes. And then a body—also lumpy—dressed in jeans and a T-shirt.

Definitely not the pretty little girl in an old-fashioned

lacy dress that she had been halfway expecting, but very clearly a boy. A boy about Neely's age, and dressed like an ordinary modern kid. An ordinary kid—who was obviously very nervous.

To her surprise Neely found herself smiling. "Hi," she said. "Where did you come from?"

The kid's eyes narrowed. "What do you mean, where did I come from?" he asked. "I live here. This is my house. My name is Hutchinson. Curtis Hutchinson. This house belongs to me—to my family, anyway."

"Really." Neely was amazed—and dismayed. "You live here?"

"Sure. Since yesterday. We came last night in a taxi. My mom and dad are still asleep." Curtis Hutchinson stared at Neely suspiciously, his pale eyes narrowing. "But they'd hear me if I yelled, and Reuben is here too. He's the watchman and he has a mean dog. And my dad has guns. A lot of guns."

"No," Grub said. "He's not."

The kid looked at Grub and then back at Neely. "What? What did he say?"

Neely waited for Grub to repeat his comment but he didn't, so she did. "He just said, 'He's not.' I guess he meant Reuben isn't here. We saw him leave."

"No," Grub said. "I meant Lion isn't mean."

But Curtis Hutchinson ignored him. To Neely he said, "You're lying. The watchman is too here. He was here last night."

"Well, he's gone now. We saw him leave in his truck.

He always goes in to town on Saturdays and we saw him go this morning, like always."

"Aha!" Curtis said, in a "now I've got you" tone of voice. " 'Like always'? Like, you always wait for the watchman to leave and then you sneak in here?" He nodded slowly, rolling out his lower lip. "You're looters, aren't you? That's what you are. Looters."

Neely felt her throat tighten. This was it. This was the beginning of arrests and policemen and judges and juries— just as she'd known there would be. Just as she'd known would happen, and then let herself forget. She took a deep breath and walked toward her accuser, her chin nobly high—Joan of Arc before the judges. As she advanced Curtis Hutchinson moved back warily. "No. We're not looters," she said with what she hoped was great dignity. "We haven't taken anything, or hurt anything. We just used to come here to play in the yard with Lion and then we found out there was an open window so we came inside. But we haven't taken anything or—"

"Sure you haven't," Curtis said in a sarcastic tone of voice. "Of course not." He screwed his face up into a cutesy, phony smile, and making his voice sugary he said, "We're innocent, officer. We just came here to play."

"Yes," Grub said, nodding and smiling. Really smiling, as if he didn't realize that Curtis was being sarcastic. "See." He gestured around the room. "See, this is where all the Hutchinson kids played. But it's been locked up for years and years and even Reuben didn't come in here, ever. And Neely and I cleaned it up. Didn't we, Neely? It was all full of dust and spiderwebs and we cleaned it up. See."

Curtis stared at Grub and then looked around the nursery—and then looked again as if he were noticing his surroundings for the first time. He walked over to Grub's circus game and stared down at it and then went on to the toy soldier battlefield below the windows. At the dollhouse he stopped and peered inside. When he had been all the way around the room he came back and stood between Grub and Neely and the door and stared at them, sticking out his round, slightly lopsided chin.

"Okay," he said. "So maybe you didn't steal anything. But you were going to, weren't you? I'm going to have you both arrested for trespassing. I'm going to call the cops and have you both arrested."

"The phones don't work," Neely said coolly. "We've tried them lots of times." Of course, there might be one that worked in Reuben's place, but she didn't mention that. To her surprise she was beginning to feel quite calm. "But if you do tell the police, just tell them we're Bradfords. Everyone around here knows the Bradfords. But right now I think we'd better go home. The key to this room is over there by the door. You can lock it back up if you want to. Come on, Grub, let's go."

For a moment it looked like the Hutchinson kid might be going to try to stop them, but then he seemed to think better of it and stepped aside. Neely headed for the stairs. They would not, she decided, go out the window. Not with *him* watching them, they wouldn't. Instead they would go right down the stairs and out the front door. They had reached the landing before she noticed the man who was standing at the foot of the stairs looking up at them.

Except for less hair and some wrinkles around his deep-set eyes, the man at the foot of the stairs looked a lot like Curtis. Like Curtis he had lumpy cheeks and a lopsided chin and jumpy light-blue eyes that flickered nervously from place to place. He was wearing a ratty old bathrobe and his feet were bare. He looked up the stairs directly at Neely and then, to her surprise, he turned and walked away. In the door to the living room he stopped and turned back.

"Curtis," he called. "Come here. Come here right now."

Curtis brushed past Neely, ran down the stairs and across the hall. The man, who was pretty obviously his father, clutched Curtis's shoulder and started talking to him in a tense, angry way. Neely couldn't hear exactly what he was saying or what Curtis said in return, but after a minute the man nodded, glanced at Grub and Neely, and then turned quickly away.

"Fine," he said to Curtis, but more loudly now. "Good. Making new friends already. What did I tell you." He patted Curtis's head in a stiff, awkward way. Then he disappeared into the living room.

Curtis met Grub and Neely at the foot of the stairs. Crossing his arms over his chest, he clutched his elbows and then glanced up at Neely and stretched his lips in a sly, foxy grin. Then he said, "Guess what I told him. I said, 'Dad, these are my new friends. I met them down on the road when I was going for a walk, and I asked them up here to see the house. Okay?' And he said it was okay."

Curtis let go of his elbows and smiled in an offhand

way, swaggering his shoulders. "My dad is a really important guy down in southern California. Really important."

"Look," Neely said. "Was that supposed to be some
kind of a joke? Telling us you were going to have us arrested and then"—she nodded toward where his father had
stood—"And then doing *that*?"

For a second Curtis stared back, smiling cockily, his
chin jutting forward. But then suddenly he ducked his head
and crossed his arms tightly over his chest again as if to
hold himself together. Looking up at Neely out of the tops
of his eyes, he said, "Yes. Yes, a joke. It was just a joke."

"Well, it wasn't funny," Neely said. "Come on, Grub.
Let's go home." They were halfway down the drive when
Curtis came running after them. "Hey, wait," he said.
"Wait a minute. Could I come with you?"

CHAPTER
23

"COME WITH US?" NEELY STARED AT CURTIS. "WE'RE GO-
ing home."

"Yeah, I know. I'll just walk with you a little way.
Okay?"

"Well, it's okay with me. Hadn't you better ask your
father?"

"Oh, he won't notice. He never notices any—" Curtis
was saying when suddenly his cocky grin faded. "Look out.
Here it comes. Here comes that dog." Grabbing Grub, he
whirled him around and held him like a shield between
himself and Lion, who was trotting toward them. Lion
growled and broke into a run.

"Stop it. He thinks you're hurting Grub," Neely yelled.
Jerking Curtis away, she stepped in front of him, spreading
her arms. As Lion came to a bouncing, snarling stop Grub
threw his arms around the dog's thick neck.

"It's okay, Lion," he said. "Down, Lion. Down."

It took a while for Grub to convince Lion that Curtis was okay and even longer to convince Curtis that it would be safe to have Lion walk with them. And even after they got under way the fuss went on, with Curtis still trying to get them to take Lion back and tie him up, and Lion still growling softly every time Curtis got too near Grub. They were, in fact, almost to the gate before Lion quit being the only subject of conversation.

But at last Neely was able to ask, "Did you say you were going to live here now, at Halcyon House?"

"Yeah, that's what"—Curtis interrupted himself to put Neely between himself and Lion—"that's what I said. My dad decided he wanted to come back here. . . ." Another pause while Curtis skittered away from Lion. "So here we are. I didn't want to come."

"Back here?" Neely asked. "Has he been here before?"

"Yeah, when he was a little kid." He shrugged nervously, keeping his eyes on Lion. "He says the place was in a lot better shape then. I guess we're going to have to fix it up a lot if we decide to stay here for a while."

They had reached the fence by then and Neely, after a moment's hesitation, led the way to the secret entrance. After all, it couldn't matter now. They'd surely not be coming back again. Once outside, with no Lion to worry about, Curtis was easier to talk to.

"You said you didn't want to come?" she asked.

Curtis shook his head. "Hell, no. I liked it where we were, and besides—"

He stopped as if he'd suddenly decided not to finish what he was saying.

Neely waited a minute before she said, "Yeah, well, that happens I guess. Like my friend Lisa. She had to move to Arizona because her dad got a new job. Is that why your dad came here? A new job, or something?"

"Yeah," Curtis said. "He's got a great job in Monterey. In a bank. He's going to have an important job in the bank. Like the manager or president, or like that."

Neely nodded. "Yeah, that's the way it goes. Like with Lisa. But I'll bet you'll like it here once you get used to it. I know I'd love to live in a place like Halcyon House."

"Well, I hate it," Curtis said. "It's too run-down and old-fashioned, and too far away from everything. And besides . . ." He stopped for a second to pick up a rock and throw it up in the air. He threw it up and caught it several times before he went on. "And besides . . . haven't you heard about Halcyon House being haunted?"

"Haunted?" Neely said. "Well, not exactly. Have you?"

"Yeah. Carmen said so. Carmen's this old woman who works for us. See, she used to be my dad's nursemaid when he was a little kid and she came here with the family a lot of times way back then, so she knows all about it. She says the servants used to talk about it all the time."

"Does Carmen still work for you?" Neely asked.

"Sure," Curtis said. "But she's not here yet. She's coming in a day or two. She's our cook now, and housekeeper. She didn't want to come here either. Because of the place being haunted. That's why I thought—" He stopped, and then went on, grinning. "That's what I thought you were when I heard you talking. Ghosts."

Neely smiled, remembering the wobbly voice behind the door. "You thought Grub and I were ghosts?" she said.

Up until then Grub had been walking on the other side of the road, not saying anything. Not that there was anything unusual about that. Grub rarely did much talking when strangers were around. But now he came over beside Neely and poked her with his elbow. "Tell him about Monica," he said.

"No, I don't think so—" Neely was saying when Curtis said, "Monica? Yeah. I remember Carmen saying something about somebody named Monica. Wasn't she the kid who died? Here at Halcyon?"

"Tell him," Grub said.

So Neely did. All about what Greta had said about pneumonia, and how some people thought she had died of something else. And then she went on to tell how there was even a story about how Monica had mysteriously disappeared.

"And the things in the trunk. Tell about that too," Grub said. "Tell about all the things that were in Monica's trunk and how people were afraid to touch them anymore after she died."

So Neely told about that, too, and Curtis seemed very interested. When she finished talking he was quiet for a minute and then he said, "Monica. Yeah. Carmen knows about her. I'm going to ask Carmen to tell me some more about Monica."

"Yeah," Neely said. "I'd like to know too. I'd sure like to find out what Carmen knows."

By that time they'd reached the crest of the hill and Neely stopped to point out their house.

"You live there? In that little old house?" Curtis said, in a scornful tone of voice, as if he thought the picturesque old Bradford house was some kind of a slum. When Neely gave him a cool stare and said yes he grinned and asked, "You got anything good to eat down there?"

Neely was definitely surprised. "Well, sure," she said. "Are you hungry?"

"Yeah. There's no food up there. Nothing except this rice and vegetable gunk the old guy, Reuben, was eating. See, he wasn't expecting us till Sunday. We were going to ride up in the car with Carmen but then we decided to fly and so we got here early."

"Oh," Neely said. "That's probably what he's doing right now. Buying some food."

Curtis's face brightened. "Yeah? You think so?" But then he frowned. "How soon do you think he'll come back?"

"Well, usually he stays all day. But maybe he'll come back sooner this time."

"Yeah, and maybe not. I think I'll eat at your house," Curtis said, and started off down the hill.

Grub and Neely looked at each other and rolled their eyes before they hurried to catch up. They were almost to their driveway when Neely heard a familiar sound and looked up to see Reuben's old blue pickup turning in off Highway One.

"Hey, look. There he is now," she said. "There's Reuben."

"Is that him?" Curtis said. "All right!" Waving his arms over his head, he jumped out into the middle of the road so quickly that Reuben had to slam on his brakes.

The last Neely and Grub saw of Curtis Hutchinson, he was climbing into the passenger seat of the pickup truck. He didn't even turn around to wave good-bye.

CHAPTER
24

"WELL," NEELY SAID WHEN REUBEN'S PICKUP HAD disappeared over the top of the hill. "That is one weird kid. Have you ever seen such a—" She stopped when she realized that Grub was no longer standing beside her. Running after him, she caught up as he trudged blindly up the driveway, his face blank and empty.

"Hey," she said. "It's all right. We couldn't have gone up there much after school started anyway. Only on Saturdays and not even then if the weather was bad. We just have to forget about it, that's all."

"I'll never forget about it," Grub said. "It was so—so fascinating." (Fascinating had been a favorite word of Neely's for a long time and Grub had picked it up lately.) "And now everything's so—tragic." (Another favorite word of Neely's.)

Grub's voice definitely had a gloom-and-doom ring to

it. "No, it isn't," Neely said quickly. "It's not as tragic as all that. It's just something that was great but now it's over."

Grub's sigh almost sounded like a sob. "We didn't even get to say good-bye," he said.

Neely thought she knew what he meant. It would have been so much better if they'd only had a little warning—and time to say good-bye—to the nursery and the library and the whole fantastically beautiful old house. And to Monica? Was that what Grub meant? To say good-bye to Monica?

To change the subject she said quickly, "Can you imagine, we went right in the house without knowing they were there, and you went down to get the key, and then we both went down to look at the guns, and nobody saw us and we didn't see any of them. And we probably walked right by the rooms they were in." The very thought made her shiver.

Grub nodded. "They were sleeping," he said.

"You'd think we would have seen something. Like a car in the driveway or—"

"He said they came in a taxi," Grub said.

"Oh, yeah. He did. But they must have a car. How can they live up there without a car? I guess Reuben could take them shopping, but how would they get to work and things like that?"

Grub only shrugged, so after a moment, Neely said, "They must have a car somewhere. Don't you think?"

"I guess so." Grub's face was still blank and stiff, but at least he was talking. "You can ask him next time we see him."

"I don't know," Neely said. "I doubt if we'll see him again."

"I think so," Grub said.

"What do you mean, you think so?"

Grub nodded slowly. "I think we'll see him again."

That night at dinner Neely told her parents about meeting Curtis—without saying exactly where. Without actually saying so, she made it sound as if they had met first in the grove. "This kid was there, and we got started talking and we met his father—and everything. They're Hutchinsons and they're going to live at Halcyon for a while," she said.

Mom and Dad were very amazed and interested and there were lots of questions about what the house looked like inside and what the furnishings were like. Mom loved to hear about things like that, so Neely went room by room telling about the most interesting things like the gorgeous pool table and the inlaid hardwood card tables in the game room.

While she was still telling about the game room, Grub said, "And the gun cupboard. Don't forget about the gun cupboard."

Neely gave him a warning frown because of the way Mom felt about having guns around the house, but then she made it all right by quickly explaining that the gun cabinet had unbreakable glass doors and a big padlock. Fortunately Mom was busy wondering if there would be any chance that she might get to see the inside of Halcyon House, now that it was occupied again. Mom had always been interested in all kinds of houses.

❖

It turned out Grub was right about seeing Curtis again. A few days later, around five o'clock in the afternoon, there was a knock on the back door of the Bradfords' house—and there he was, Curtis Hutchinson in person.

"Hi," he said, holding out two wrinkled paper bags. He was smiling, but instead of his usual cocky grin, this one was squinty-eyed and nervous, like a dog that doesn't know whether to expect a pat or a kick. "Hi. I brought you these. You left them up at the house."

Neely laughed. "Well, thanks, but no thanks. They're probably pretty rotten by now."

"Well, actually, I ate the cookies," Curtis said. "But not the sandwiches. I don't like tuna. The sandwiches are still in there."

Neely took the bags to the garbage pail and just a minute later her mother came out to see who had knocked. "Well, who's this, Neely?" she asked.

"This is Curtis Hutchinson, Mom," Neely said. "This is my mother, Connie Bradford. I told you about meeting Curtis last Saturday."

"Well, well. Welcome to Halcyon Hill, Curtis," Mom said. "It's nice to know someone will be living in that beautiful old home again."

"Yeah, for a while at least. The old dump is pretty run-down right now but my dad will have it fixed up before long. You know, get rid of a lot of the old-fashioned junk. Put in new bathrooms and stuff like that. It won't be too bad once that's done."

"No, I suppose not," Mom said. "Anyway, we're glad you're here. Neely says your father came back to Halcyon because he has a job at a bank. I was wondering if it might be where we do our banking."

"Oh." Curtis looked startled. "Well, he may not take the bank job after all. He may just rest for a while. He's been kind of sick lately. Or maybe he'll just write his book. He's been working on this great book lately and he practically has it sold already. He's a great writer. There are a lot of great writers in our family."

"Why, that's wonderful," Mom said. "How exciting." Her lips were twitching and she was careful not to catch Neely's eye, as if she were afraid they both might laugh if she did. Neely knew what was funny, of course. Mom always thought it was funny when people did what she called ego-tripping . . . strutting around and trying to sound important.

After Mom went back in the house Curtis still hung around, walking around the yard and looking at Grub's chickens and rabbits and turtles. Grub came out, too, and followed them around, but he didn't say much. Curtis talked a lot. He asked about what school Neely went to and it turned out he would be in the sixth grade too. He also talked about the private school he'd gone to in Beverly Hills and how maybe he'd go to public school this year just for a change, but he didn't think he'd like it.

"Well, maybe you'll be in my class then," Neely said. It was an interesting thought. She wondered what the other kids would make of him. He would not, she decided, be a big hit. Not if he kept on ego-tripping about his rich and famous family and other embarrassing things like that.

"Well, I guess I'd better go," he said finally. And then to Neely's surprise, "Why don't you come too? Up to Halcyon House, I mean."

"Well, I don't think we could right now," Neely said. "We're going to be having dinner in an hour or two."

"Oh." Curtis looked disappointed. "Well, come tomorrow then. Okay? Come up tomorrow."

It was Grub who said okay first. Poking Neely, who was still speechless with surprise, Grub said, "Okay. Huh, Neely? We can come tomorrow. Can't we?"

Neely said she guessed they could.

CHAPTER
25

THERE WERE A COUPLE OF REASONS WHY NEELY DIDN'T really want to go back to Halcyon House. The most important one concerned the nursery, and it felt, she had to admit, a lot like jealousy. Somehow it really hurt to think about what Curtis probably had been doing to the nursery.

Especially to the dollhouse. Not that he was apt to have actually played with it, but she wouldn't put it past him to ruin things just for the fun of it. She pictured the lovely cherrywood chairs and tables with missing legs, and perhaps even the beautiful doll family with broken heads and torn clothing. She hated even to imagine it.

The other reason was that going back to Halcyon House under the circumstances just might be a little risky. Of course, Curtis had lied to his father before, to protect her and Grub, but what if he got mad at them, or just changed his mind? What if he got them up there and then told his father that he'd been lying and that Grub and Neely were actually trespassers?

On the other side of the argument there was the fact that Grub definitely wanted to go. There was no doubt about that. Ever since Saturday he'd been, if not in a full fledged gloom-and-doom attack, not very far from it. He'd been spending a lot of time in his room since then, reading or staring out the window. When Neely asked him he always said he was okay, or that he was just sad because it was August. August always made Grub sad because September came next and the start of school. But this time Grub's depression wasn't just the usual beginning-of-school blues, because right after Curtis showed up and invited them back to Halcyon he suddenly became a lot more like his normal self.

Neely tried to warn him that it wouldn't be the same. "The nursery is his now, and he can do anything he wants to with all the stuff in there," she told him.

"I know," Grub said. "I know that. I just want to . . . go there again."

"Well, okay," she said. "We'll go. But remember, it's going to be very different now."

The first big difference was that they were able to enter the estate grounds by way of the grand front gate. Curtis had said it would be unlocked and it was. And the next one was that Lion didn't come running to meet them.

"Let's go look in his doghouse." Grub's face was puckered with worry. "Maybe he's just asleep."

Neely was afraid there was more to it than that. Lion had never been too sound asleep to come to meet them before. But she agreed to go look. It felt funny walking right past Reuben's house on a Thursday. Neely almost expected him to burst out through the front door shouting at them, but he apparently wasn't at home. Lion was however. When they got to his doghouse, there he was all right, lying at the end of a long chain. When he saw Grub he went into such convulsions of joy he almost tied himself in knots. Grub and Lion were still climbing all over each other when a voice said, "I knew it. I knew that poor animal was harmless if you treated him right."

It turned out to be Carmen, the old woman who had been Curtis's father's nursemaid, and was now, according to Curtis, the family's cook and housekeeper. She had seen them, she said, from the kitchen window and had come out to say hello. Carmen was short and sturdy, and gloomy in a cheerful sort of way, as if she thought everything was pretty bad but she was too used to it to let it get her down.

"Guess you're the Bradford children," she said to Neely as she led the way into the huge old kitchen. "Curtis said you'd be coming to play today but I didn't know whether to believe him. You can't always tell with Curtis. Come on in. Real nice to have company in this lonely old ruin. Terrible old wreck of a place. Not like it used to be, I can tell you."

That was intriguing—the "used to be." The thought of talking to someone who knew so much about the way Halcyon used to be fascinated Neely. She had several questions in mind, but to her surprise Grub asked one first—several actually. Stepping in front of Neely he asked, "Why is Lion tied up? Did he do something bad? Can I untie him?"

Carmen put her hands on her hips and stood for a

moment staring down at Grub while her grumpy frown gradually got mixed up with a halfway smile. "No," she said, "he didn't do anything bad that I know of, but I don't think you'd better untie him. He's just tied up because Curtis and his father are afraid of dogs."

She studied Grub's face for a moment more before she said, "He's only tied up during the daytime, dearie. Mr. Hutchinson lets Reuben turn him loose as soon as it gets dark."

"But—" Grub was beginning when Curtis suddenly appeared in the kitchen door.

"Hi," he said, "you're late. Come on. Let's go upstairs."

As they were leaving the room Carmen called after them, "Don't forget to introduce your friends to your mother, Curtis. You promised you would. She's in the game room."

"Oh, yeah," he said. He changed directions and headed for the front of the house. In the entry hall he stopped and said, "Wait till you meet my mom. She's really something."

"Something?" Neely asked.

"Yeah. Like glamorous and beautiful. And young. Like, she looks a hell of a lot younger than your mom, for instance."

"Well, she probably is younger," Neely said. "My parents had another family that were almost grown up before they got around to Grub and me." She started to explain about Aaron and Julie and Lucie, but Curtis didn't seem interested. Instead he just went on about his mother.

"She was working in Hollywood when she met my

dad," he said. "She was thinking about being in the movies. She could have been if she'd wanted to. She was about to get discovered when she met my dad."

When they got to the game room Curtis's mother was sitting at one of the card tables smoking a cigarette and playing solitaire. She was wearing a purple velvet robe with silver embroidery, her hair was so blond it was almost white and she had on a lot of makeup. She looked young all right, and glamorous maybe, but not exactly what Neely would call beautiful.

"Well, would you look at this," she said when she looked up from her cards and saw them. "Here you are, just like Curtis said you'd be. The new little girlfriend and her brother. Come over here and let me look at you."

The way she rolled her eyes and smiled when she said "girlfriend" made it obvious she was making a big mushy deal out of it. Which was pretty ridiculous, but it didn't bother Neely all that much. She'd met adults before who thought it was pretty funny to make comments like that about kids.

When kids made unfunny jokes Neely tended to handle it with a very long, very cool stare, but with adults she usually pretended she hadn't heard. That's what she did this time. Going over to the card table, she put out her hand. "Good morning, Mrs. Hutchinson," she said. "I'm glad to meet you. My name is Cornelia Bradford and this is my brother, Gregory."

"My, how poised and polite," Mrs. Hutchinson said. "Curtis, you could certainly take lessons from this young lady. And, oh my. Look at this."

Curtis's mother was staring at Grub. Neely had a sinking feeling she knew what was going to happen—Mrs. Hutchinson was about to start making a fuss over how gorgeous Grub was.

"Oh my," Mrs. Hutchinson said again. "What a handsome child. What a heartbreaker. My dear," she said to Neely, "have your parents looked into getting an agent for this child? They should, you know. He is simply outrageous."

Neely knew Grub was hating it. His eyes said so.

"Mrs. Hutchinson," she said firmly. "Please don't fuss over Grub. He doesn't like it." She turned to Curtis to say something like "Let's go"—and wound up not saying anything. Something in his face made her forget what she'd meant to say. It wasn't till later, when she'd had time to think, that she figured it out. Actually it wasn't too hard to understand why homely old Curtis had been looking so angry.

CHAPTER
26

NEELY WAS CURIOUS. ON THE WAY UPSTAIRS SHE GLANCED at Curtis once or twice. His eyes were squinted and his lower lip was jutting out. When Neely said, "Your mom is pretty glamorous all right," he only shrugged and made a snorting noise.

A minute later he said, "*She* thinks she is anyway." He was breathing deeply. "The Hutchinsons don't think so though. They think she's cheap. That's what my cousins say. They say nobody wanted my dad to marry her."

Neely didn't answer. She didn't know what to say—and besides, they turned the corner just about then and there was Curtis's father coming through a door at the end of the hall. He was dressed this time in a shirt and khaki pants but the same ratty old bathrobe was still draped around his shoulders. When Neely started toward him to say hello, he turned and went back through the same door.

Neely looked at Curtis questioningly but he only

shrugged and said, "He doesn't like to talk to people when he's working on his book. Writers are that way."

"Oh yeah, I guess so," Neely said. "My dad knows some writers. Some of them are pretty strange at times. What is your dad's book going to be about?"

"Survival, mostly," Curtis said. "It's mostly about survival. You know. About how to go build a fortress in the mountains and protect yourself when a war comes or a revolution. My dad's always been real interested in survival."

Neely might have asked some more questions about the survival book, but they'd reached the nursery by then and there were other things to think about.

While Curtis was unlocking the door she hung back—bracing herself for how bad things might be inside. As Grub ran into the room eagerly, practically vibrating with excitement, she followed slowly—and almost froze in amazement. It looked exactly the same. Nothing had been changed in any way. The circus and battleground were just as Grub had left them, and the toy soldier who had been chosen for the role of kidnapper still lay in front of the window of the dollhouse right where Grub had dropped it.

"Hasn't anybody been here?" she finally managed to ask. "Since we were here, I mean?"

Curtis looked uncomfortable—and then tried to cover it with his phony supercool act. "Naw. I just didn't feel like it. I had too much else to do."

"You haven't been back here at all . . . since Saturday?" Neely asked.

"Sure I have. I came in and got the key—and your lunches, didn't I?" Curtis said.

"And you locked it back up. Why did you lock it back up?"

"Carmen told me to. And besides, why should I want to come in here? I don't play with this kind of kid stuff."

So Neely's worries about what Curtis had been doing in the nursery had apparently been unnecessary because Curtis "didn't play with kid stuff." At least that's what he said. But when Neely suggested that maybe he'd like to go somewhere else to play he quickly said no. And before very long he seemed to be having a great time making the toy soldiers have an extremely bloody battle. Grub played with him for a while and then went back to the circus game and, Neely noticed, to his invisible playmate. And while Grub played and whispered, Curtis went on mowing down whole regiments of soldiers.

Neely had been fooling around with the dollhouse—making up stuff about the kidnapping in between thinking about other things—when suddenly she realized what had happened. Or what hadn't happened—and why. Curtis had simply been afraid. He'd been afraid to be alone in the nursery. She was pretty sure she was right, but she decided to check it out.

Neely put the mother doll back on the bed where she'd been weeping for her kidnapped child, took pity on her and produced her baby from where he'd been hidden by the kidnappers and put him back in his mother's arms, then got up and went over to the battlefield and sat down beside Curtis.

When Curtis looked up from firing off a line of cannons she said, "Did you get a chance to talk to Carmen about Monica?"

Curtis's eyes narrowed suspiciously. "Yeah," he said. "I talked to her. Why?"

"I don't know. Just curious, I guess. What did she say?"

Curtis looked at Neely through narrowed eyes. But then his desire to be the one who knew something important obviously got the better of his suspicious nature. Putting down a cannon, he turned around, grinning in a strange, almost gloating way. "Well," he said, "at first she said it had all happened a long time before she was ever here and it was all just talk, but *then*"—he paused for dramatic effect—"then she said that nobody knew for sure . . . *but* the Monica kid was probably murdered."

Neely gasped. She'd been wanting something mysterious and exciting, but not something as bad as that. It was too unbelievably awful. She was still staring at Curtis in speechless surprise when she became vaguely aware that Grub was standing behind her. "Murdered?" she finally managed to ask. "How? Who murdered her?"

Curtis looked up at Grub and then at Neely, obviously pleased at the effect his story was having. "Well, see," he said, settling into the telling, "this old woman told Carmen that all the servants were *told* Monica died of some kind of disease, but it had really been, like, an accident. What really happened was that she'd fallen out of a window. *And*, she also said that some of the servants thought it hadn't just been an accident . . . like maybe she was pushed, or something."

For a long moment Neely was silent, her mind racing. She heard Grub whisper something under his breath, but before she could ask him what he'd said, Curtis went on, "Carmen said this one old servant who'd been Monica's nanny said that some of the other kids had pushed her because they hated her."

"Hated her?" Neely asked. "Why would they hate her?"

Curtis shrugged. "I don't know. Carmen says that Monica's nanny said it was because the grown-ups liked her best. Especially their grandfather who had all the money liked her best, so she always got all the best stuff." He grinned and shrugged. "But maybe it was just because she was a dirty little snitch. I have a cousin who's like that." He laughed noisily. "I might push *her* out a window if I got a chance."

Neely gave him a cold stare and after a moment he clutched his elbows and grinned sheepishly. "Just joking," he said.

On the way home that day Neely kept thinking about what Carmen had told Curtis. Grub must have been thinking, too, because he was very quiet. They were almost to the gate when she remembered that she'd wanted to ask him what he'd whispered while Curtis was talking.

"Grub," she said. "What did you say when Curtis said Monica fell out a window?"

"I said, 'that window,'" Grub said. "I said, 'maybe out that big window.'"

Neely thought she knew what window Grub meant. All the rest of the way home she kept picturing the big window behind the bandstand in the ballroom and wondering how it happened. Wondering if the two iron bars that protected the lower half of the window had been there when Monica fell or if they'd been put there afterward when it was too late. Too late at least for Monica. Because it didn't really seem possible that anyone could fall clear over the bars—unless they were pushed pretty hard.

She wanted to ask Grub what he thought, but he didn't seem to want to talk about it anymore. Several times when she asked him something he just shook his head, but finally when she asked, "Do *you* think someone pushed Monica?" he nodded slowly and said, "Someone. Someone pushed her."

Neely stopped walking and grabbed Grub's arms and shook him. "Who?" she demanded. "Who pushed her?"

Grub turned his face away. "I don't know," he said.

Neely shook him harder. "Then how do you know she was pushed?" she said.

But Grub didn't answer. He pulled away and ran down the hill toward home.

CHAPTER
27

Just a couple of days later the phone rang early in the morning and it was Curtis. "Hey," he said, "our phones are working. You want my number?" And after Neely said "Sure" and wrote it down, he went on, "Hey, why don't you come up for a while today?"

"Well . . ." Neely hesitated. She had been thinking about going into town with Dad to spend the day with Mimi. But when she said so, Curtis said, "Well, how about tomorrow then? Or the day after? Or this Friday?"

The problem was that Neely still wasn't sure whether she wanted to keep going back to Halcyon House. Or to be more specific, she was sure and she wasn't.

She wanted to go back, on the one hand, because Halcyon was still an intriguing place, even though the arrival of Curtis and his family had spoiled it in some ways. There was still, after all, the unsolved mystery of Monica and the possibility that there were more fascinating facts to be discovered about her. And she really wanted to find out more about the murder thing, from Carmen or maybe even from Curtis.

And then, too, there were probably many other interesting things to find out about other star-crossed Hutchinsons, as well. She was really intrigued by the thought of all those other old Hutchinson mysteries that might yet be uncovered.

And, she had to admit, she was curious about Curtis and his family too. She'd never known a person like Curtis who flip-flopped from one kind of personality to another in such an unpredictable way. Or anyone whose father didn't have to work except *maybe* to spend his time writing a book about survival. (Neely wasn't sure she believed that story any more than she believed the bank manager one.) Or whose mother sat around all day in a velvet robe playing solitaire. There were, she decided, a few mysteries about the present-day Hutchinsons to be solved as well. And mysteries, particularly tragic ones, had always been hard for Neely to resist.

She also was tempted to say yes because Grub wanted to go back to Halcyon so much. And at the moment, the moment being August, with the beginning of school coming nearer and nearer, Grub really needed something to take his mind off his worries.

Grub had always hated for school to start and this year he hated it more than usual. Most people, and especially Mom, couldn't understand it because, unlike most kids who hate school, Grub was a very good student. Neely, herself, couldn't understand it entirely.

When she asked him about it once he said something like, "I don't know. I guess I just don't know how to do it right."

"Do what right?" Neely had asked. "You're great at school. You're fantastic at reading, and you know more history and geography than most high school kids, and you're even pretty good at math. What do you mean you don't know how to do it?"

Grub sighed and turned away. But a moment later he said, "It's everything else I'm not good at. Like doing things the right way."

"What things? What kinds of things don't you do right?"

"Everything," Grub said. "Everything . . . like saying funny things and laughing real loud." And after he'd thought some more he added, "And yelling and pushing."

She understood part of that, particularly the part about yelling and pushing. Watching a bunch of second-grade boys at recess, you couldn't help but understand how important it was to be able to yell and push, not to mention slug and kick. Grub had just never learned how to do that kind of thing, and he probably never would.

It wasn't that the other kids were mean to Grub. At least, not as mean as they usually were to people who were different. She didn't know why for sure except that, even though he was different, there wasn't anything about Grub that really invited meanness—he wasn't pushy, or hard to get along with, or ugly. And another reason no one was ever very mean to Grub was because they knew that if they were, they'd have Neely to deal with. And perhaps that explained why Grub was even more depressed than usual about school starting this time. Because this year, for the first time, he and Neely would be going to different schools.

But whatever the reason, Grub was right on the edge of a serious case of gloom and doom, and Neely knew that having a visit to Halcyon to look forward to would help.

So there were some good reasons to say yes to Curtis's invitation. Some good solid reasons. And the arguments on the other side were much less solid. In fact there was nothing much Neely could put her finger on—just a vague, uneasy feeling that something wasn't right.

But after Curtis changed the date three or four times— "Well, how about tomorrow then? Or the day after? Or this Friday?"—she finally found herself saying yes.

"Sure," she said. "Friday's okay. I'm not doing anything on Friday."

After she hung up she went to find Grub and tell him, and when she did he went from gloomy to cheerful in half a minute. It wasn't until she was back in her room that she realized that Curtis hadn't said anything about Grub being invited too.

"Not that it matters," she told herself. "He probably just forgot to mention Grub." She threw herself down on her bed and opened her book to where she'd been reading when the phone rang.

"Yeah," she said. "He just took it for granted that I'd know that Grub was invited too. That's probably it. That better be it, Mr. Curtis Hutchinson."

CHAPTER
28

On friday when neely and grub arrived at halcyon they went directly to the doghouse for a visit with poor old Lion. Grub was still rolling around on the ground with his arms wrapped around his head to keep Lion from licking his face, when the kitchen door opened and Curtis came out. Neely went to meet him.

"Hi," she said. "Here we are, right on time."

Curtis wasn't smiling. "Yeah," he said. "So I see. You and your shadow. Who invited your shadow?"

Neely gave him a long stare. "What do you mean?" she asked. "You asked both of us, didn't you? Because if you didn't we can just go right—"

Curtis grabbed his elbows, squeezed his arms against his chest, and ducked his head, looking at Neely out of the tops of his eyes. "All right," he said. "All right. He's invited. He's . . ." His shoulders lifted in a jerky shudder.

"Look at him. How can he let that mutt slobber all over him like that?"

While Curtis stared at Grub and Lion, Neely watched him curiously. "I guess you just don't like dogs," she said.

"I hate them," he said. "I'd like to kill them all. I did kill one once."

"You what?"

"I shot one. With my dad's gun." Curtis's chin was jutting out again. "He tried to bite me so I shot him."

Neely stared at him. It might just be another of Curtis's lies. She hoped so. Giving him a really disgusted look she said, "I hope you're joking."

He looked away, up at the sky and then down at his arms, which were still hugging his chest. "Yeah," he said. "I'm joking. Hey . . . what do you want to do? Want to play pool?"

"Sure," Neely said. "I don't know how, but I guess I can learn."

When Grub tore himself away from Lion and came over, wiping his face, Curtis didn't say hello. Instead he just turned to Neely and said, "Okay. Let's go."

As they were going down the hall Neely asked Curtis where his parents and Carmen were.

"Carmen's around here somewhere," he said. "In her room I think. My mom and dad are in Monterey. To see a doctor. My dad has this doctor's appointment every Friday."

"Oh. Is he sick?" Neely asked.

"Well, sort of. It's his nerves. He's very nervous," Curtis said. "He doesn't think he needs to go, but he has to because he said he would. He promised he'd see this doctor every week if we came here to live."

That was interesting. Neely wanted to know who Mr. Hutchinson had promised and why he had to, but before she could ask they passed the stairs and Grub grabbed her arm. "Aren't we going up to the nursery?" he asked. When Neely told him they were going to play pool instead he looked disappointed.

"Look," Neely said. "Could Grub go play in the nursery?"

"Sure," Curtis said. "Feel free, pal. You go right on up to the nursery. Don't forget to get the key. It's in the kitchen now. On one of those hooks near the door."

"Why do you keep it locked?" Neely asked.

"I don't. It's Carmen. Carmen keeps it locked." He shrugged, and then as Grub started up the stairs he called after him, "Hey, kid. Say hello to Monica for me."

Neely was surprised. She hadn't told him about Grub's "playing with Monica" game and she was sure Grub hadn't either. "Why did you say that?" she asked when Grub had disappeared up the stairs.

"Say what?"

"About Grub's saying hello to Monica."

"Oh, that. Because that's where she's supposed to be. The Monica ghost. Carmen said so. I asked her to go in the nursery with me, and she went in and looked around but she wouldn't stay. She said that she'd never been there before. Like, not even when she used to come here when my dad was a kid. That room was always locked even then.

135

Nobody ever went in there. So that must be why. Because it was haunted."

Neely was a little bit shocked. While Curtis got down the pool cues and showed her how to hold them, she had a hard time keeping her mind on what he was saying. She kept thinking about Grub up there all alone in what was, maybe, a haunted room.

She hadn't thought of it that way before—even that time when she'd held the sampler like a magic charm between the palms of her hands and concentrated on Monica so hard she'd seen her, or at least had almost seen her. Even then she hadn't connected the nursery and Monica with words like "haunted" or "ghost." Somehow she hadn't ever felt that way about Monica. But now the word "haunted" kept popping into her mind, making it hard for her to concentrate on what Curtis was saying. But after a while she began to get interested in learning to play pool.

She wasn't too bad at it. Not great, but almost as good as Curtis and he'd had a lot more practice. She almost won once or twice, and one time she almost certainly would have except that Curtis changed the rules at the last minute. After he'd changed them two or three more times she decided she was going to read up on the rules before she tried to play pool with Curtis again.

Once when she'd kind of given up on trying to keep Curtis from cheating, she decided not even to watch him taking his turn. Instead she wandered off into the library. She hadn't been there since the Hutchinsons moved in, and before that it had been her favorite room, next to the nursery, of course. She hadn't had a chance to look at the family portrait over the fireplace since she'd learned about Monica.

Standing in front of the fireplace, she stared up at the picture of the man with the slick, dark hair, the pale-faced woman, the two boys and the little girl. Mostly she looked at the pretty little girl and the two sleek-faced brothers with their heavy brows and blank, dark eyes.

This time there was something about the picture that made her feel uneasy, as if the peaceful calm she'd always felt in the library had been spoiled. But later, sitting in the alcove near the shelf of books about girls and horses, it came back again. A comforted feeling, as if she were in a place where someone could be safe and happy. She was still sitting in the alcove when Curtis came looking for her.

"Hey," he said. "I won. I ran the whole table."

Neely wasn't a bit surprised. An hour or so later when she announced she was getting a pool headache, Curtis tried to talk her into a game of chess, or badminton, but she said "no, thanks" and started up the stairs to get Grub. Curtis followed her, still arguing about it being too early to go home.

When they got to the nursery Neely noticed the door wasn't quite closed and she was just putting out her hand to open it when Curtis grabbed her arm and whispered, "Shhh. Listen. Someone's talking."

Neely listened and, of course, it was Grub. Grub's voice talking steadily but not quite loud enough for her to hear the exact words. She shoved the door open and went in. Grub was sitting on the floor playing with the model barn-yard. He had the dog in his hand and he was making him round up a herd of cows, sheep, and pigs. When he saw Neely and Curtis he jumped to his feet and said, "Hi. Is it time to go?"

Then, as he bent down to put the dog back in the barnyard, Neely saw him smile and whisper something—something that looked like good-bye.

Neely glanced at Curtis. She wasn't sure if he realized that Grub had been telling Monica good-bye, but from the look on his face she thought maybe he did.

CHAPTER
29

CURTIS KEPT ON PHONING. SOMETIMES HE JUST WANTED to talk. Usually he talked about the school he went to in Beverly Hills and about the places he used to go with his friends. Places like Universal Studios and Knott's Berry Farm and Disneyland. And how all his friends had lots of money but he had the most money so he usually got to decide what they were going to do. And what great times he'd had and how much more fun it was than living out here on the edge of nowhere. But on Friday when he called, the last Friday before school started, Neely could tell right away by the sound of his voice that something was wrong. It was almost as if he'd been crying.

"What's the matter?" she asked.

"Matter? What makes you think something's the matter?" he said in an argumentative tone of voice, and then before she even could answer he said, "Yeah. You're right. Something's the matter but I don't want to talk about it."

There was a gulping sound and then he went on, "Hey, can you come up?"

Neely suppressed a sigh. She really didn't want to say yes, but at the same time she couldn't help feeling sorry for poor old Curtis. Not to mention curious about what had happened to upset him so much. She wondered if it might be something to do with Monica.

"Well, I don't know . . ." she was saying when he added, "Both of you. Bring Grub, too, if you want to."

"Well, I'll see," Neely said. "I'll see if—"

Just then something tapped her on the shoulder and she turned to see Grub standing behind her, smiling and nodding his head.

"Okay," she said, shrugging off her misgivings. "We'll see you in about an hour. Okay?"

Curtis and Grub said okay in unison.

When they got to Halcyon House that day Grub again insisted on going first to visit Lion. But this time, while Grub and Lion were still wrestling, Reuben came out of his little house. He was wearing his familiar old floppy hat and his face was as worn and saggy as his overalls. Standing on his front step he stared at the giggling Grub and the bouncy, tail-wagging Lion. And Neely stared at him.

Watching Reuben made her feel creepy without exactly knowing why, except that he'd been a kind of bogeyman for so long—for all those months when the only real threat to Grub and Neely's secret visits to Halcyon was the danger of being caught by the fierce-looking old man. But now, as Neely watched, Reuben's face broke into a different pattern of cliffs and valleys and his mouth stretched into what was unmistakably a grin. Neely watched in surprise, and then went over and held out her hand.

"Hi," she said. "I'm Neely Bradford. And that's Grub." She smiled and shrugged. "He likes dogs a lot."

Reuben nodded. "I see," he said. "They are old friends, are they not? Your brother and Lion?"

Neely gulped. Did that mean that Reuben knew about all their secret visits to Halcyon? She certainly hoped not. "Old friends?" she asked. "Well, sort of. Some people make old friends in a hurry."

Reuben turned his surprising, saggy smile toward Neely. "Quite true," he said slowly. Then he went on staring at Grub and Lion until, at the sound of a slamming door, he glanced up, turned on his heel, and disappeared into his cottage.

It was Curtis who had slammed the door as he emerged from the kitchen carrying a net and two badminton racquets. He was wearing baggy khaki shorts, there were blotchy red spots on his face, and his eyes were even jumpier than usual. A few minutes later when Grub had disappeared in the direction of the nursery, and Neely and Curtis were heading for the tennis court, Neely asked again if anything was the matter.

Curtis shrugged and didn't answer, but when they got to the court and Neely was helping him string up the badminton net, he suddenly said, "It's my stupid father. It's my stupid paranoid father that's the matter." His eyes were narrowed to angry slits and some muscles around the corners of his mouth were twitching.

"Paranoid?"

"Yeah. You know what that means?"

Neely thought she had a general idea but before she could answer Curtis went on, "That means you think everyone's out to get you. Unless you get them first." Curtis's voice was getting higher and tighter. "What it means is you're nuts. Crazy. Psycho!"

He was practically shrieking before he stopped. Neither one said anything for a minute or two. Then Neely said, "Oh. Is that why he has all those guns? Because he's worried about someone trying to get him?"

"Yeah. That's part of it. And all that survival stuff too. He just thinks somebody's going to start a revolution any minute and kill everybody unless you kill them first. And what's even stupider, he thinks that if I go into Monterey with him and go to the aquarium or walk around Cannery Row or something while he's at the doctor's I'll get kidnapped or something."

"Oh," Neely said. After a moment's thought she asked, "Couldn't your mom go to the aquarium with you, so you wouldn't have to go alone?"

"No. She didn't want to go anywhere today. She's still in bed."

Neely looked at her watch. "In bed? Is she sick or something?"

"No, she's not sick. She just doesn't feel like getting up. Sometimes she doesn't get up all day. She just lies there and drinks chardonnay and plays solitaire."

That was a pretty amazing thought. For a moment Neely tried to picture her own mother lying in bed all day . . . and gave up. It was just too completely unimaginable.

When she'd finished getting her end of the net tied up she asked, "Who told you your father was paranoid?"

Curtis's frown made Neely think of an angry cat.

"Okay, okay," she said. "Forget it." She smiled apologetically. "Sorry I asked. Okay?"

Curtis clutched his elbows and the frown gradually faded. "Everybody told me," he said suddenly. "All my cousins. All my stupid, fat-headed cousins. And Carmen. And my mom too. Everybody says so. That's the reason he has to go to the shrink every Friday. My uncle made him promise to go to the shrink or we couldn't live here—in this house."

"Your uncle? How come your uncle gets to tell your father what to do?"

"Because he's the trustee. That means he gets to say when my father gets money from the estate. And when he doesn't. That's why we had to come here to live. Because my crummy uncle decided the trust wouldn't pay our rent anymore, so we had to live here or nowhere." Curtis threw a bird up into the air and smashed it so hard it went clear off the court and into the tall weeds.

While they were hunting for the bird Neely was careful not to ask any more questions. And she certainly didn't mention that Curtis had just as much as admitted that all his big stories about his father and why he and his family had come to Halcyon House had been lies.

When they started playing she let Curtis win sometimes, even though she could have won every game if she'd wanted to. Curtis wasn't much of a badminton player. He puffed and panted and every few minutes he fell over his

143

own feet. When he missed a shot he got angry at the racquet or the net, or sometimes at the bird.

Once when the bird got stuck in a tree he threw a rock at it to get it loose and the rock bounced back and hit him in the head. It wasn't a very big rock and it couldn't have hurt all that much, but when he finally got the bird down he stomped on it until it was completely flat.

"Hey," Neely said, laughing. "What are you doing that for? Now we can't play anymore."

Curtis stopped glaring at the smashed bird and gave Neely a cocky grin. "Sure we can," he said, and pulled another bird out of his pocket. "My serve. Are you ready?" Then he threw the squashed bird into the bushes and started serving.

For a while after that he was pretty cheerful, as if squashing the bird had made him feel better. He was still in a pretty good mood when Neely said she'd better go get Grub and head for home.

"Hey," he said as they were going up the stairs to the second floor. "All that stuff about my dad was a lie. Okay? I was lying about him." He ducked his head and grinned his twitchy grin. "I'm a good liar," he said. Which wasn't exactly news to Neely.

CHAPTER
30

ON THE FIRST DAY OF SCHOOL GRUB WALKED DOWN TO the bus stop with Neely even though his bus, the one that went to Carmel River School, wasn't due for quite a while.

"I'll go back up to the house before your bus comes," he said. "I just want to wait with you for a while. Like old times." So Neely swallowed a grin and said, "Okay. Like old times," and started talking about Mrs. Kingman who would be his teacher for the third grade. They were still talking when Carmen's beat-up old Buick came down the hill and turned out onto Highway One. She pulled up at the bus stop and Curtis got out.

"Hi," Neely said. She was surprised that Curtis was going to ride the bus. She'd heard that new kids from outside the district had to come with their parents on the first day.

Curtis said hi and then, nodding toward Grub, he

asked, "What's he doing here? I thought you said the bus for elementary school kids doesn't come till later."

Neely waved at Carmen as she backed and turned the car around before she answered Curtis's question. "He was just keeping me company for a while. How come you're riding the bus today? Won't your parents have to go to the office to fill out the transfer forms and stuff like that?"

"No," Curtis said. "My dad called the school. And I've got all the papers from my old school with me. I didn't want my folks taking me to school like I was some wimpy little elementary school dweeb. Who needs it?"

Neely didn't say anything about how Curtis was just one summer away from being an "elementary school dweeb" himself, but she let her grin suggest it. Then she pulled Grub aside and went on telling him about Mrs. Kingman.

Fortunately Neely had been in Mrs. Kingman's class herself three years before, so she was able to tell Grub how great she was and how she always made her class work at being a "community," which basically meant they all had to get along and be nice to each other, or else. Hearing about being part of a community seemed to cheer Grub up for a minute, but then he sighed and frowned.

"I probably won't do it right," he said. "You probably have to go around talking to people and saying the right kinds of things and . . ." He sighed again.

Neely smiled. "What kinds of things?" she asked.

Grub shrugged. "I don't *know*. That's why I don't do it right."

Neely was still suggesting some things Grub might say

that morning when he met people he hadn't seen since last year, when she glanced over to where Curtis was leaning against the school bus sign. He'd taken some papers out of his backpack and was pretending to be looking through them, but he was really watching Grub and Neely out of the corners of his squinted eyes. She was about to tell him what she and Grub were talking about and see if he had any suggestions, when the middle-school bus came into view and Grub dashed off up the hill.

Curtis got on the bus first and went way to the back, and Neely sat near the front beside Patty Denton, a seventh grader whom she'd known for a long time. But at the next stop Curtis moved closer. He seemed to be trying to listen to what Neely was saying, but when she tried to introduce him to Patty he looked out the window and pretended he hadn't heard her talking to him.

So Neely went on talking to Patty, and after the next stop to Benjy and Justin and Marta. She hadn't seen any of them much since school was out, so there was lots to talk about. And Justin, who was always pretty funny, started telling about a crazy skateboard contest he'd won, and everyone laughed and shrieked until the bus driver told them to cool it or he would stop the bus until everybody shut up.

Once, when the laughter had died down for a minute, Neely said, "Hey, everybody. Meet my new neighbor, Curtis. Curtis, these loudmouths are Benjy and Marta and Justin."

Everyone said something and Justin stood up and did a fancy bow and said, "Hi, new neighbor, Curtis," and everyone laughed. Curtis said "hi" in a stiff, uneasy way and then looked away, pretending to see something interesting out the window. Justin was starting to do a "well, what kind of a nerd do we have here?" bit, rolling his eyes and mugging, so Neely said quickly, "Curtis is a Hutchinson. You know. A Halcyon House Hutchinson."

That got their attention, just as she'd known it would.

"Oh, yeah," Patty said in a very impressed tone of voice. "You live in that huge old mansion up on the hill?"

Suddenly Curtis did one of his weird personality flip-flops. Standing up, he swaggered up the aisle, ignoring the bus driver who yelled at him to sit down, and plopped himself down in the seat behind Neely and Patty.

"Yeah," he began, sticking out his chin and waggling his shoulders the way he always did when he was trying to be supercool. "I guess we're going to live in the old shack for a while. We've got some other houses, in Beverly Hills and Hollywood and like that, but my dad decided somebody needed to fix up the old Halcyon place, so we . . ."

Neely was listening with a sinking feeling. She'd always hated it when people did totally embarrassing things, even when it was only in a book or a movie. And an ego-tripping Curtis was definitely embarrassing. But, fortunately, the bus turned in at the school grounds about then and everybody stopped listening and started waving to friends and yelling, "Hey, there's old Dino. Hi, Dinosaur Man!" and "Look at Taylor. Hey, dude, where'd you get those bummie threads?" and things like that. In the excitement everybody, including Neely, forgot all about Curtis.

The rest of that day and the rest of the week, too, were pretty busy. There were dozens of old friends to catch up on gossip with. And lots of new things to get used to, like having core classes, and different schedules on different days of the week. And there were choices to be made, such as what enrichment class to take. Like drama, for instance, which was what Neely decided on. That was going to amuse Lucie, Neely thought, and she imagined Lucie saying, "Oh, come on, Neely. Don't you think you're *dramatic* enough without taking a class in it?"

And on Friday there was the election of sixth-grade representatives. There happened to be a lot of Neely's old friends from Carmel River School in Mr. Hardcastle's core class, which was probably the reason she won the election.

So, even though it turned out that Curtis was also in Mr. Hardcastle's core class, Neely was too busy to spend much time noticing how he was doing. But, now and then, in class or sometimes in the hall between classes she would look up and there he'd be, looking in her direction. When that happened she always said "hi" or at least nodded and smiled even though he always looked away quickly, pretending he hadn't seen her.

But then, on Thursday afternoon while Neely and some other kids were waiting to get on the school bus, Patty Denton suddenly poked Neely and whispered something in her ear.

"What?" Neely said. "I didn't hear you."

"Shhh." Patty hissed a little louder, "He's staring at you again. That nerdy Hutchinson dude is staring at you again." She giggled and rolled her eyes. "I think it's love." She giggled. "True, true love." And after that she kept poking Neely and whispering, "True, true love," every time she happened to see Curtis, which was several times a day, since he seemed to show up amazingly often.

Neely just ignored Patty's "true love" nonsense. But she did think about Curtis sometimes. Once or twice at home, sitting in the window seat or curled up on her bed with a book, she thought about him a little. She had to admit that he seemed to follow her around at school quite a lot. She didn't really believe it was "true love" though, and she certainly didn't want it to be. It was just a slightly interesting idea. After all, no one had ever been madly in love with her before. At least not that she'd noticed.

Chapter
31

THAT FIRST WEEKEND AFTER THE START OF SCHOOL THERE happened to be an early rain, so when Curtis called up on Saturday morning Neely was able to say, "I don't know. It's raining pretty hard. I don't think we can—"

"What if Carmen came down to pick you up?" Curtis interrupted.

"She wouldn't, would she?"

"Sure she would," Curtis said. "She will if I tell her to. She'll be there in fifteen minutes. Okay?"

The "okay" sounded like a question but he hung up so fast that Neely didn't get a chance even to think about it, let alone answer. But when she went to the kitchen to talk to Mom about it, Grub was already there putting on his rubber boots.

"I already asked," he said, grinning. "Mom said okay. She said no at first but when I said they were coming to pick us up she said okay."

"How did you know Carmen was coming?" Neely asked.

"I heard you talking," Grub said, grinning. "I picked up the hall phone and listened."

"You did, did you!" Neely grabbed Grub's ear and twisted it. "You know what happens to little creeps who listen to other people's phone conversations? They get their little ears pulled off."

Grub giggled, pulled away, and dashed out onto the back porch. A second later he was back with Neely's boots. "Hurry up," he said. "She's almost here." Neely was just putting on the second boot when there was the sound of a car motor and the muddy old Buick pulled into the back-yard. As Neely and Grub ran out through the rain Carmen leaned over and opened the door on the passenger side.

"Where's Curtis?" Neely asked as she got into the front seat with Carmen.

Carmen laughed her short, barking laugh. "He's baking cookies," she said. "Believe it or not, he's baking cookies."

Neely found it hard to believe, all right.

"Yes, indeed," Carmen went on. "A couple of hours ago he started insisting that I bake some cookies because he was expecting guests."

"Expecting guests?" Neely grinned. "You mean he was expecting Grub and me a couple of hours ago? He didn't even ask us till about twenty minutes ago."

Carmen made a snorting noise. "That's our Curtis," she said. "And then, just as I get the first batch in the oven he comes running in insisting that I have to come down here and pick you up. Immediately. So at the moment he's sitting in front of the oven holding two hot pads and waiting for the timer to go off. Or at least he'd better be or he's going to have some lumps of charcoal to serve his guests."

Neely looked back at Grub and they both giggled. Somehow the picture of Curtis sitting in front of the oven clutching the hot pads was pretty funny. But then she thought of something else and quit laughing. The unfunny part was that she didn't even wonder why no one asked Curtis's mother or father to take over the cookie baking. She'd learned enough about Curtis's family by now to know why that probably wasn't a possibility.

A minute later Carmen glanced over at Neely and when Neely smiled she smiled back—frowning at the same time. Not many people can do that but it seemed to be a specialty of Carmen's. Still smile-frowning, she shifted gears and tromped on the gas pedal as the car slid backward on the muddy road.

"Neely," she said suddenly, "about Curtis. He sometimes has these strong—well, violent really—enthusiasms about things . . . or people. It's happened before."

"Enthusiasms?" Neely was puzzled.

Carmen nodded. "Enthusiasms. Obsessions almost." Carmen wasn't looking at Neely now. Instead she was staring intently ahead at the muddy road, her face tense and squinty-eyed. "I—I worry about him," she went on finally. "He's had a hard time of it, you know."

"I know." Neely was feeling very uneasy. "That is, I can imagine."

Carmen shifted again and reached over and patted Neely's hand. "I'm sure you can," she said. "I'm sure you can imagine how hard it's been for him. He's hurt and angry. Sometimes he's terribly angry. You mustn't forget that. You mustn't forget that Curtis can be terribly . . ." She paused again and glanced at Neely and then quickly away. "Angry," she said again softly—but it somehow sounded as if she'd meant to say something else.

Neely was still wondering what other word Carmen had been planning to use when suddenly she changed the subject entirely and started asking Neely about her first week at school.

"I hear you won an election," she said.

"Well, just for sixth-grade representative," Neely said. "Sixth graders don't get elected to really important things at a middle school because it's their first year."

"Curtis seemed to think it was important," Carmen said, and then she asked Grub, "How about you, Grubbie? How was your first week?"

Grub leaned forward and put his chin on the back of the front seat and looked at Carmen in the rearview mirror.

"Okay, I guess," he said. "I'm in third grade now." He stopped and thought for a moment, chewing on his lower lip. Then he smiled brightly and said, "I only have nine more grades to go."

Just at that moment the Buick slid to a stop in front of the iron gates of the Halcyon estate. Only half the gate was open.

"Oh, dear," Carmen said. "The gate. I left it open but the wind must have blown it shut."

"I'll get it," Grub said, and jumped out of the backseat. The gate was heavy and as Grub tugged his feet slipped and slid on the muddy road. Carmen and Neely leaned forward watching. Grub gave up on pulling and ran around to the other side and tried pushing. The gate began to move and he looked over his shoulder grinning triumphantly. Beside her, Neely heard Carmen catch her breath in a strange wobbly sigh.

"Such a lovely child," she said. "You must watch over him, Neely. You must protect your little brother."

Neely felt a strange shudder travel down the back of her neck. "Why?" she started to say. "What do you—"

But at that moment Grub opened the door and jumped back into the car smelling of rain and wet hair. Carmen was saying, "My, my. What a strong young man you are to manage that heavy gate in all that rain."

Grub looked proud and pleased. "It's a good thing I wore my boots," he said.

As Neely glanced back at his wet and shiny face the shudder came again, trembling slowly down her spine.

CHAPTER
32

THE COLD WIND-DRIVEN RAIN, DRIPPING DOWN THE STONE walls and trickling across the windows of Halcyon House, looked like sad, gray tears. But inside the huge old kitchen the air was warm and dry and smelled like a bakery. Apparently Curtis had done a good job. In the middle of the kitchen table there was a platter of nicely browned oatmeal cookies.

However, the hot chocolate he'd decided to add to the menu hadn't been quite as successful. The top of the huge old-fashioned eight-burner stove was awash in sticky boiled milk. While Carmen cleaned up the mess, she and Curtis argued about the proper way to make hot chocolate.

It was too bad about the ruined hot chocolate, but as far as Neely was concerned it did come in handy as a topic of conversation. At least while Carmen and Curtis argued about spilled milk Neely didn't have to think of things to say, which at that particular moment might have been a problem because her mind kept skidding off the track and back onto the subject of Grub in danger.

In between listening to Curtis and Carmen's argument she kept hearing Carmen's voice saying "You must protect your little brother." The thing was, she did protect Grub all she could. She always had. But apparently Carmen felt she hadn't done it well enough. Or that she would need to do it better. Curtis and Carmen were still fussing at each other when Neely suddenly realized what Carmen had been talking about.

It was the nursery, of course. The nursery, and the fact that she had allowed Grub to play there by himself while she and Curtis played pool or badminton.

Curtis had said that Carmen thought the nursery was haunted, and of course she would think it was dangerous for Grub to be there all alone. Or—Neely again felt the shiver threaten the back of her neck—all alone perhaps, except for . . . Monica. It would be almost impossible, she knew, to keep Grub away from the nursery, but at least she could make sure he no longer went there by himself.

So a little later when the cookie eating was over and Carmen had taken herself off, still grumbling, to her own room, Neely immediately turned down Curtis's suggestion of a game of pool.

"I'm tired of pool," she said. "Why can't we do something in the nursery?"

Curtis's lumpy unformed face tightened into an angry scowl. "Why?" he said. "What could we do in that crummy place?"

Neely shrugged. "I don't know. There's all that great stuff in there. There's all kinds of—"

The scowl deepened and Curtis's voice went high-pitched and sarcastic. "I get it. You want to play with the piggies and horseys. Sure. You just want to play Farmer in the Dell with little ol' Grubbie."

Neely sighed and stood up. "Grub," she said. "I'm beginning to feel like a nice refreshing walk in the rain. Come on, let's go home."

Grub stared at Neely and she looked back, trying to make her eyes say she was sorry but that it was necessary, and at the same time watching to see what his reaction would be. With his big eyes wide open with shocked surprise, and with all the damp curls hanging down across his forehead, he looked so much like something on an old-fashioned valentine that Neely found herself smiling just a little . . . until she noticed that Curtis was watching her. After a second Grub nodded sadly, got to his feet, and headed for the door. Neely followed and they were almost there when Curtis yelled, "Wait. Wait a minute. Okay. You win. We'll do something in that stupid old babies' play-room."

In the nursery Grub immediately went into his favorite corner with the toy circus, while Curtis wandered around trying out windup toys and musical instruments. Neely wandered, too, for a minute, but she knew immediately where she was heading and it didn't take her long to get there—the dollhouse. She really didn't know how much she'd missed it until she was there. Without even meaning to she put out her hand to touch things—the beautiful sideboard, the grand oval dining table, and the delicate rocking chair.

The gorgeous old grandfather clock that could actually tell time had run down. She picked it up, checked her watch, set the time, and then wound the key. When it was ticking she put it back in the living room, and then decided it might look better in the front hall. That meant she had to move a sideboard and when that was done she decided to do a complete job and rearrange the furniture in every room.

This time she didn't pretend she was Monica, or at least not exactly. It somehow didn't seem natural with Curtis there in the room making weird noises on the accordion. But she did find herself trying to imagine where Monica might have put a particular piece of furniture, before she decided on each new location. The rearranging took quite a lot of time and, of course, she stopped now and then to check on Grub.

Grub had set up the three rings of the circus and like always he was talking softly as he played. Neely looked to see if Curtis had noticed but he seemed to be too busy with the accordion. Besides, she told herself, even if he did notice he'd probably only think that Grub was making the circus people talk to each other. After all, lots of little kids do that kind of thing when they play.

She was still rearranging furniture when the nursery door burst open and Mrs. Hutchinson came in. She was wearing a satin robe that looked like a Japanese kimono, her blond hair needed combing, and her voice was slurred and mumbly.

"Well, well, well," she said. "Isn't this touching? Children playing again in the old family nursery. How sweet."

She started around the room in her high-heeled slippers, wobbling a little when she stopped to look at the old toys and musical instruments, and almost falling down when she bent to peer into the dollhouse. When she'd regained her balance she grabbed up the dining room cabinet, tipping it so all the dishes in the glass-fronted cupboards slid to one side. Neely reached out to catch them if they fell.

"Oops." Mrs. Hutchinson smiled apologetically and put the sideboard down. "Must be more careful, mustn't we? Worth a fortune nowadays, beautiful old doll furniture like that. Absolute fortune."

She then went on around the room, stopping briefly to inspect the accordion Curtis was holding. Making a face, she put her fingers in her ears. "So that's what was making that awful noise," she said. "I thought something was dying."

When Curtis's mother got to Grub's corner she immediately began to make another embarrassing fuss over him. She mussed his hair and then, putting her hand under his chin, she tried to turn his face up toward hers. Grub blushed and squirmed and tried to get away. After she finally turned him loose and teetered to the door, she turned to blow kisses in his direction before she disappeared down the hall.

As soon as Curtis's mother had gone they all went back to what they'd been doing before. But not long afterward Curtis put down the accordion and went over to sit on the floor next to Grub. The next time Neely checked he was holding one of the animals and he and Grub were talking softly together. Neely smiled. Curtis seemed to be the one playing Farmer in the Dell, or whatever, with Grubbie. The next time she checked they were getting to their feet and heading for the door.

"Curtis wants to show me something in the ballroom," Grub said. "We'll be right back."

Neely might have gone, too, but she had only one more room to rearrange and she didn't want to leave the job unfinished. She had almost completed the last room when a disturbing thought occurred to her. It was the first time she'd been in the nursery all alone. And maybe if, as Carmen seemed to think, something might happen when Grub was there all alone, perhaps it might happen to anyone who was there all by themselves.

Still holding the dollhouse baby crib in her hands, Neely began to walk slowly around the room, stopping now and then to listen for phantom voices and watch for the glowing lights or swirls of heavy mist that you always read about in ghost stories.

Nothing happened. No mists and no voices. Not even when she was standing in Grub's favorite corner where he usually played his games of circus or farmyard with his invisible companion. She was still standing there, thinking that it was no use, that nothing was going to happen, when it suddenly occurred to her that quite a bit of time had passed and perhaps she'd better go see what Grub and Curtis were doing in the ballroom. Quickly putting the baby crib back in the dollhouse, she ran up the stairs to the third floor.

They were in the ballroom all right, standing together on the little bandstand in front of the big picture window. Curtis had his hand on Grub's shoulder and they seemed to be looking out at the endless view. When Neely let the door slam Curtis took his hand off Grub's shoulder and started to thump on one of the drums. Grub jumped down from the platform and ran. Dashing down the long stretch of ballroom floor as if he were in some kind of race, he skidded to a stop a few feet away from where Neely was standing.

"Hi," Curtis called from the bandstand. "I was showing Grub the drum set. I was telling him about how we could start our own band."

On the way downstairs Curtis babbled away about his idea to start an orchestra using the drum set and some of the instruments from the nursery. "I was showing Grub where we'd all sit on the bandstand," he said. Grub didn't say anything at all but, of course, there was nothing too unusual about that.

CHAPTER
33

THAT NIGHT, PROPPED UP AGAINST THE HEADBOARD OF her bed in a comfortable nest of pillows, Neely stared at page twenty-seven of a really interesting book for about thirty minutes without reading a single word. She stared at the page and thought, instead, about what Carmen had said about protecting Grub.

She'd hoped to see Carmen again before she left Halcyon House, to ask her exactly what she'd meant, but there was no one in the kitchen when Neely and Grub and Curtis went back downstairs. And since the rain had stopped she couldn't very well suggest that Carmen ought to drive them home. So she'd had to go on guessing what Carmen meant when she said "watch over your little brother."

Neely was sure—well, almost sure—that the warning concerned the nursery and Monica. Obviously Carmen believed in ghosts in general and in the Monica ghost in particular. But that didn't explain why she thought

Grub especially needed protection. Why would the Monica ghost—why would anybody, ghost or not—want to hurt Grub? And if someone or something did want to hurt him, what could Neely do to prevent it?

There were other questions too. Questions with no answers or with too many answers. So for at least half an hour Neely stared at page twenty-seven and thought and thought without coming to any conclusions, except a couple of halfway ones. One halfway conclusion was that Carmen was probably wrong about Grub being in any special danger. After all, Neely herself had been alone in the nursery and absolutely nothing had happened.

But the other conclusion was that maybe the best solution would be for her and Grub simply to stop going to Halcyon House altogether. She didn't come to any definite decision about that—she didn't want to, really—but it was, she told herself, something to consider.

It was the very next morning at breakfast when, right out of the blue, Mom said, "Neely, your father and I have been discussing it and we think perhaps we'd better put an end to these Halcyon House visits."

Neely looked up from her buckwheat pancakes, stunned into silence. For a long moment she stared at her mother while she tried to decide what she was going to say.

She was feeling shocked and indignant—and more than a little surprised that she felt this way since it was, after all, exactly what she had almost decided herself. But she *was* indignant. It just wasn't fair of Mom simply to cut things off without any warning when there were so many mysteries—mysteries about Monica and all the rest of the star-crossed Hutchinsons—yet to be solved. It just wasn't fair. And then, glancing over at Grub, Neely was reminded of another important reason why Halcyon shouldn't be made off-limits. Which, of course, was that it still mattered so much to Grub.

"Why?" she asked her mother in a resentful tone of voice. "Why shouldn't we go to Halcyon when we're asked?"

"Because," Mom said, "your father and I haven't met the Hutchinsons and it's beginning to look as if we're not going to. I called the other day and talked to their house-keeper, I guess it was—"

"Carmen," Grub and Neely said in unison.

"Yes, Carmen. And she seemed very nice, but she said she'd ask Mrs. Hutchinson to return my call, and no one has called back as yet. And you know, Neely, that your father and I have always insisted on knowing a little about the people who spend a lot of time with our kids."

"Dad?" Neely appealed to her father.

He shook his head, smiling. "Oh, I quite agree with your mother," he said. "At least for the time being, until we can find out a bit more about the family."

"Oh, is that all?" Neely said. "Well, what do you want to know about them? Maybe I can tell you."

Mom smiled. "Well, I don't know if that will entirely solve the problem, but there are some things I'm curious about. They do seem to be a rather strange bunch. For instance, the fact that nobody seems to work. And why has this particular part of the family come to live at Halcyon after all these years?"

Neely glanced at Grub. His eyes were wide and pleading. She gave him a reassuring smile, took a deep breath, and began. She wouldn't lie, but she would answer carefully. Very carefully. "Well," she said, "I don't think there's anything so strange about them not working. People like the Hutchinsons don't have to, I guess. Curtis said something about a trust fund. And besides, Mr. Hutchinson has been sick. I guess he sort of moved here to rest and get well."

"Sick?" Mom asked. "What kind of illness?"

"I'm not sure what the symptoms are," Neely said, which was pretty much the truth. "But he sees a doctor a lot. He goes to Monterey to see a doctor."

"It's not catching," Grub said. "It's not chicken pox or diphtheria."

Both Mom and Dad laughed, which was a good sign. And when they dropped the subject of the strange things about the Hutchinsons, Neely felt that maybe she was winning. Especially when Mom started asking about what she and Grub did when they were at Halcyon. At that point the conversation switched to pool and badminton and all the wonderful toys in the great old nursery.

Neely talked quite a bit about the beautiful dollhouse because she knew that would appeal to Mom. Mom always stopped to look at dollhouses in toy stores, and sometimes she talked about the one she'd had when she was a little girl. Houses, of all sizes, had always been important to Mom.

By the time breakfast was over the verdict was in and it seemed that Halcyon was not forbidden after all. At least not right away.

"Well, that does sound like a lot of fun," Mom had finally said. "So we'll see. Perhaps something can be arranged to make it possible for us to meet the Hutchinsons before too long."

"And in the meantime . . . ?" Neely asked.

"We'll see," Mom said.

Neely was on her way to her room a few minutes later when Grub dashed after her and almost knocked her down with a giant bear hug.

"Turn loose, you klutz," Neely said, prying his arms loose and pinning him against the wall. "You trying to kill me, or what?"

"No." He giggled. "It was just a hug." He laughed again, a crowing, gurgling laugh like a tickled baby, then he ducked away and kind of danced into his room. Grub was like that when he was happy.

Neely stood there looking at his door for several seconds before she went on to her room and sat down on the bed. Grub was obviously out-of-his-skull delighted because she had made it possible for him to keep on going to Halcyon House. She hoped she wouldn't be sorry. She hoped he wouldn't be. Suddenly her shoulders lifted in a quick, sharp shiver.

CHAPTER
34

THE NEXT TIME CURTIS CALLED UP TO INVITE NEELY AND Grub to Halcyon there were new things to take into consideration, one of them being that any particular visit might be their last one. At any point Mom and Dad might give up on getting acquainted with the Hutchinsons and make Halcyon House off-limits forever. Or, on the other hand, they might somehow manage to meet the Hutchinsons, in which case the outcome would probably be pretty much the same. Either way it would be the end of going to Halcyon, since a successful meeting between Connie Bradford and Joyce Hutchinson was pretty impossible to imagine.

After thinking and worrying for quite a long time, Neely decided that maybe it was all for the best. The visits would stop—very soon. Just as soon, in fact, as she had one more chance to talk to Carmen. One chance to find out a little bit more about the mystery of Monica, not to mention exactly what Carmen had meant when she warned Neely to watch over Grub.

So the next Saturday when Curtis called up she said okay—for what was probably the last time. But of course she didn't mention that fact to Curtis—or to Grub.

It was beautiful fall weather that Saturday morning and as Neely and Grub climbed up Halcyon Hill in the soft sunshine, the gentle warmth and the absolutely calm air made Neely think about the meaning of the word *halcyon*, and how it came from a myth about a beautiful bird. About a bird whose nesting season was always a time of peace and calm.

Trudging up the road through the soft fall warmth, with a humming, smiling Grub skipping along beside her, was like a brief halcyon moment. A very brief moment, since there was something she was going to have to do before the day was over that would take away a lot of peace and tranquility, at least where Grub was concerned.

She was going to have to tell him that this was their last visit to Halcyon, and the sooner the better, since he would hate it even more if he didn't have time to say good-bye. Taking a deep breath, she began: "I'm getting a little bored with going to Halcyon. Aren't you?"

"Bored?" Grub stopped skipping, thought for a moment, and then nodded slowly. "Yes. A little, I guess. But we can't stop. We can't stop going there."

"Why not? Why can't we?"

"Because . . . it would be lonely there without us."

Neely stopped walking and stared at Grub, and he stared back, wide-eyed, smiling just a little.

Neely put her hands on her hips. "Grubbie. You say the weirdest things sometimes. Who'd be lonely?"

"Lion," Grub said promptly, and then after a pause, "and Carmen, and Curtis and . . ." He stopped, letting his gaze drift off into space.

Neely didn't say "and Monica," even though it was right at the very tip of her tongue. She didn't know why but somehow she didn't think she should. But even though she didn't say "and Monica" she was certainly thinking it—and she was pretty sure that Grub knew that she was.

The next step, of course, was to tell Grub that this would be their last visit—and try to explain why. But somehow she couldn't do it. Not now. Not in the midst of this beautiful halcyon moment. So instead of going on with what she had planned to say she suggested playing Hinky Pinky, one of Grub's favorite word games, to get his mind off the subject. To get both their minds off the subject, really.

They had gone through the gate and were on their way up the long curve to Halcyon House, and Neely had just grabbed Grub and started to tickle him to pay him back for turning one of his Hinky Pinky answers into a kind of insult. (The clue he'd given was "a slimy girl" and his answer turned out to be "eely Neely.") Grub was very ticklish, so he was squealing and giggling and Neely was laughing, too, when she looked up and there was Curtis watching them. He was wearing his baggy shorts and a faded blue T-shirt and carrying a pool stick. As he stared at Grub and Neely, he kept swinging the stick around in front of him.

"Oh, hi." Neely laughed. She let go of Grub and he bounced away.

"Hi, Curtis," Grub said. He was still giggling but Curtis stared at him without even smiling. Then he turned and walked toward the house, switching the bushes beside the road with the pool stick as he went. Grub looked at Neely and they both did a questioning shrug, and then Neely hurried to catch up. When she said, "Thanks for coming down to meet us," Curtis only glared.

"I didn't come down to meet you," he said in a surly tone of voice. "I just went down to unlock the gate."

Neely laughed. "Okay. Then thanks for unlocking the gate."

He only shrugged but at least he looked at her for a moment. A minute later he said, "Well, my dad's gone."

"Gone?" Neely said. "Where? Where'd he go?"

"To this kind of mental-health place in San Francisco, with some other people who go to his shrink. They're having, like, this group session kind of thing where they all sit around and talk about their problems."

"Oh." Neely nodded. "Well, that sounds good. Lucie, you know, my sister, said they did something like that in one of her psychology classes. They all sat around and talked about stuff like that. She said it was kind of fun."

"Yeah, sure," Curtis said. "Lots of fun."

No one said anything more for a while, but a little later Curtis stopped hitting things with his stick and by the time they got to the house he seemed to be in a little better mood. As they were going up the wide stone steps of the veranda he asked Neely if she wanted to play pool. She didn't really, but since he was in such a bad mood she decided she'd better not make it worse by arguing. She would play pool, that is, if she could talk Grub into staying in the game room, too, instead of going on alone to the nursery. And that, she knew, wouldn't be easy.

It took some fast talking, first of all, to get Curtis to agree to let Grub try his hand at playing pool, and some even faster talking to get Grub to think he wanted to.

"We'll all take turns playing pool for a while," she told them, "and then we'll all three go up to the nursery. Okay?"

At last she got some grudging okays, but it soon became obvious that neither Grub nor Curtis was having a very good time. Grub was really too short to use the cue stick very well and Curtis refused to teach him how to do it, as he had with Neely. Instead, he kept making disgusted snorting noises when Neely tried to show Grub how to hold the stick. Neely was about to give up and suggest they all go upstairs when she realized that this might be her best chance to have a private conversation with Carmen. Particularly since it might be better to leave Grub in the game room rather than in the nursery. So the next time it was Grub's turn to play against Curtis, Neely announced that she was terribly thirsty.

"You two guys play for a while," she said. "I'll be back as soon as I get a drink. I'll just run down to the kitchen. Is Carmen there, Curtis?"

Curtis was so busy watching Grub that he didn't hear Neely's question, at least not right away. Grub was standing on tiptoe and the end of the cue stick was almost touching the end of his nose. It did look pretty funny but Curtis wasn't laughing. Staring through narrowed eyes, he seemed to be so intent on what Grub was doing that Neely had to ask again about Carmen before he heard her and answered.

"Yeah, sure," he said finally. "She's in the kitchen."

But when Neely got to the kitchen Carmen was nowhere in sight. Neely wandered around for a few minutes, looking out the windows to see if Carmen had gone out to the garbage pail, or maybe to feed Lion. But there was no sign of her there either.

Right at that moment, standing there in the middle of the kitchen, Neely considered giving up and going back to the game room. Which might very well be giving up on her last chance to talk to Carmen about Grub—and about Monica as well. She hated to give up, but what else could she do. Unless . . .

Having suddenly decided to see if Carmen was in her room, she ran up the back stairs and down the long, dim hall—but when she knocked on Carmen's door there was no answer. After knocking twice more Neely reluctantly gave up and went back downstairs, wondering why people who were almost always around insisted on disappearing when you most desperately needed to see them. She was in the lower hallway and starting toward the game room when she decided to take one last look in the kitchen.

This time, as she entered the room, Carmen was coming through the door from the pantries. She was wearing a big apron and yellow rubber gloves, and carrying a large tin pail full of soapy water.

"Hi, Carmen," Neely said. "I've been looking all over

for you. I guess you're pretty busy but I wonder if I could talk to you?"

"Why, hello, Neely," Carmen said. "I didn't know you were here." She glanced around and then said, "And Grub. Is Grub here too?"

"Oh, he's all right," Neely said. "He's not in the nursery. He's in the game room. And Curtis is with him."

Carmen nodded. "With Curtis?"

"Yes," Neely said. "They're playing pool, more or less."

Carmen was frowning. "More or less?" she asked.

Neely grinned. "Yeah. Grub hasn't ever played and he's not too good at it, and Curtis isn't exactly in one of his better moods."

Carmen's answering smile was distant, preoccupied, and as Neely watched it changed into something that looked like sudden fear. Carmen started across the kitchen and as she passed the table she reached out to put down the bucket of soapy water—but she didn't reach quite far enough. Neely made a dive to catch the falling bucket but she was too late. It hit the floor with a loud clatter and a great splash of soapy water. Carmen didn't even look back.

CHAPTER
35

THE GAME ROOM WAS EMPTY. THE CUE STICKS WERE STILL lying on the table among scattered balls, but there was no sign of Grub or Curtis. Carmen looked around quickly and then hurried across the room and into the library. As Neely followed close behind her, she found herself fighting against a slowly rising tide of anxiety. There was no one in the library. From above the mantel Monica and her family looked out across a silent, empty room.

Back in the game room Carmen leaned for a moment against the pool table. She was breathing hard, her hands still in the yellow rubber gloves, clutching the table railing. Neely stared at the gloved hands, her mind racing in confused circles. Something about the strangeness of the wet rubber gloves on the beautiful inlaid wood was terribly frightening, turning the trickle of anxiety into a sudden flood of terror.

"What is it?" she asked frantically. "What's the matter, Carmen?"

"Where are they?" Carmen said, but not to Neely. Her eyes were rolled upward and somehow the question sounded like a prayer. "Where could they have . . ." Her voice died away, and turning suddenly she almost ran across the room to the corner beyond the fireplace. Following close behind her, Neely watched as if in a trance while a yellow-gloved hand reached out to touch the open latch of the gun cabinet. The padlock was missing. Neely stared at Carmen—and then followed her horrified gaze to where three guns hung against the back wall of the cabinet. Only three. One of the handguns was missing.

"Curtis!" Carmen shouted so loudly and so suddenly that Neely recoiled with shock. There was no answer. Hurrying, almost running, Carmen retraced her steps, back across the room, through the entry hall and out onto the veranda, while Neely ran beside her still asking, "What is it? What's the matter? What's happening, Carmen?"

But Carmen didn't answer. Standing on the steps, she cupped her hands around her mouth and shouted first in one direction and then in another. "Curtis! Curtis, you come here. You come here this minute."

"Carmen! What's the matter?" Someone else was calling now from inside the house, and through the open doorway Neely was able to see Joyce Hutchinson teetering down the stairs in her high-heeled slippers . . . down the stairs and across the veranda, blinking in the sunlight, her old/young face looking smeared and frightened. She grabbed Carmen's arm and shook her. "What's the matter, Carmen? What is the matter?

"It's Curtis," Carmen said. "He has a gun. And Grub. Grub's with him."

"A gun." Joyce Hutchinson's face looked frozen. "How could he have a gun? The cabinet is locked."

"No. It was open. He must have found the key."

"Oh no." Joyce's hands went up to her mouth. "Oh no," she said again, and then something halfway muffled that sounded like "not again." Stumbling down the stairs, she ran clumsily out across the lawn, her long robe floating out behind her. As she ran she shouted, "Curtis. Curtis. Where are you, baby?" And Carmen ran, too, in the opposite direction.

Left alone on the veranda, Neely started after Carmen and then Joyce . . . and then stopped altogether. After a moment's thought she turned back to the house. Back to the house and up the stairs, three steps at a time, all the way up the first flight and the second and into the ballroom. Into an empty ballroom where, to her immense relief, the window behind the bandstand still seemed to be sealed shut, the glass unbroken.

But she had to be sure. Running down the long floor, Neely staggered across the bandstand, gasping for breath, and leaned on the top bar—the bar that had been put in place after Monica fell . . . Monica. Neely stared down the steep drop to the rocks below and whispered, "Monica." And standing there by the window, saying Monica's name, she suddenly knew what she could do.

Knew, as suddenly and as surely as if someone had whispered it in her ear, exactly what to do to find Grub.

She ran again then, back across the ballroom, down two flights of stairs, through the back hall and kitchen, dashing across slippery hardwood floors and taking stairs in flying leaps. And then out the kitchen door to where Lion strained against his chain, facing down the path that led to the rose garden. The moment that Neely unsnapped the chain from his collar he sprang forward, growling as he ran, and disappeared down the path.

Neely followed him, gasping and panting now, but still running as hard as she could. But Lion was much faster and she was soon left far behind. She had just left the rose garden and was turning toward the stable when she heard the shot.

CHAPTER
36

As neely burst through the stable door, out of the sunshine and into the dim light of the central corridor, she could see only that something was moving toward her. Something that growled and, at the same time, sobbed and pleaded, "Come on, Lion. Let's go. Come on."

As the large, confused shape moved closer and her eyes became accustomed to the light, she saw with a great rush of relief that it was Grub. Grub, tugging on Lion's collar while Lion, growling fiercely, tried to pull away and go back. Neely grabbed for the collar and together they managed to pull the big dog down the corridor and out through the stable door. Outside, in the bright sunlight, Neely could see that Grub's face was pale, his eyes huge and wet with tears.

"Grub," she gasped. "What happened? Where's Curtis?"

"Back there," Grub whispered. He let go of Lion's collar, closed the stable door, and leaned against it. "In one of the stalls. He tried to shoot Lion but he missed and then he tried again but it didn't go off, and then he hid in one of the stalls." Hearing his name, Lion pressed against Grub, trying to lick his face.

"Oh, Grub." Neely suddenly found her voice so shaky she could barely talk. She pushed Lion aside and clutched Grub's shoulders, shaking and hugging him at the same time. She was still hugging when suddenly Carmen was there, too, and a moment later Joyce.

Carmen's gray hair had fallen down around her flushed face and she was gasping with exhaustion. "Grub," she whispered and suddenly reeled, staggered and almost fell. Neely let go of Grub and jumped to help Carmen regain her balance.

"Grub," Carmen whispered again, reaching out for him with her yellow-gloved hands. "Thank God." And then, "Curtis? Where's Curtis?"

Neely pointed. "In there. In one of the stalls. He's all right."

Still gasping and panting, Carmen staggered into the stable, and Joyce, who had said nothing at all except for some strange whimpering noises, followed her.

Left alone, Neely and Grub stared at each other. "Grub," Neely said, "what happened? Why did Curtis have the gun?"

Grub shook his head. "I don't know. I don't know why. But I think he was—"

"What's going on here?" It was Reuben, his wrinkled

face tightened and pinched with concern. "What happened? Thought I heard a shot."

"Yes," Neely said. "It was Curtis. Curtis had a gun. But nobody got shot."

"He missed," Grub said. "He missed Lion."

Reuben stared at Grub. Then he knelt down and ran his hands over Lion's head and body. When he stood back up he turned to look at the stable door. "Crazy kid," he said. "Ought to be locked up." Taking off his belt he looped it through Lion's collar and led him back down the path toward the house.

It was quiet then and from inside the stable there was the sound of voices. Carmen's and then Joyce's speaking softly and pleadingly. And then there was shouting. Curtis shouting, "No, no. I won't come out. He'll kill me. That dog will kill me."

Neely pushed the door open and went in. "Stay here," she told Grub. "I'll be right back." She was well into the stable before she could see Carmen and Joyce standing in front of a stall door. And she was even closer before she saw Curtis's hands clutching the top of the door.

"He's gone," Neely said. "Lion's gone. Reuben came and took him away. You can come out now."

The door opened slowly and Curtis came out. He was clutching his chest, his head hanging. "That dog tried to kill me," he said in a high-pitched voice. "He tried to kill me."

"Curtis," his mother said, "where is the gun?"

"In there," Curtis nodded back toward the stall. "It didn't work. The stupid thing didn't work."

Carmen tried to put her arms around Curtis but he shoved her away. "The gun, Curtis." Her voice was sad and stern. "Why did you have the gun?"

Curtis's head came up slowly. He was smiling. "I found the key," he said. "Dad thought he had it hid where I'd never find it, but I did."

"But why?" his mother asked in a shaky voice. "Why did you have the gun? What were you going to do with it?"

Curtis looked around. His eyes focused on Grub, who was standing in the stable door, silhouetted against the light. Lowering his voice to a whisper he said, "It was Grub. He wanted to see it. He begged and begged me to show him how to shoot it. So I was going to show him, but then someone let that stupid dog loose and it almost killed me." Curtis put his arms around his mother and leaned against her, hiding his face. "He was going to kill me, Mom," he said.

Joyce Hutchinson patted her son's head. Then she turned to Carmen and said, "See? It's all right. He's all right. He was just trying to be nice to the little boy."

Grub and Neely walked home. Carmen offered to drive them but Curtis didn't want her to. "Don't go away, Carmen," he said, his face twisted into a tragic mask. "I need you to be here. I'm sick. I'm sick because of that dog." The pitiful face changed into a reproachful one. "Besides, you just want to talk to them. You can talk to them some other time, when I'm feeling better." He turned to his mother.

"Tell Carmen she can't go," he begged. And Mrs. Hutchinson did tell Carmen she couldn't go.

"He needs someone with him, Carmen," she said. "And I'm just going to have to go up and lie down this minute. I'm not feeling at all well myself. I'm sure Curtis's little friends won't mind walking home."

So Neely and Grub walked home just as they had so many times before, but this time was very different. It was different because Neely knew now, without the slightest doubt, that it was the last time. The last time they would ever walk home from Halcyon House. And it was different, too, because of the way Grub was acting. Usually, coming home from a visit to Halcyon, Grub was happy—bouncing, skipping, humming, happy. But now he was silent and pale, his eyes dark and clouded. When Neely tried to talk to him he only shook his head.

But she kept trying. "Grub, I know you don't feel like talking, but you can just answer yes or no. Can't you do that?"

Grub shook his head.

"Just yes or no," Neely insisted. "Did you really ask Curtis if you could see the gun? Just yes or no. Please, Grub."

But Grub would only shake his head.

Mom was in the kitchen when they got home. "Well," she said. "You're home early. I wasn't expecting you for a while." Then she stopped talking and her eyes followed Grub as he walked across the room and disappeared down the hall. "Something wrong with Grubbie?" she asked Neely.

Neely took a deep breath, biting her lip, and thought. The decision came quickly. She would burn the bridges— all the bridges to Halcyon House. She would make certain that she could never change her mind and go back, and most of all, that Grub could never go back. She would tell about the gun. Knowing how her mother felt about guns she knew that would be enough.

She pulled back a chair and sat down at the kitchen table. "Mom," she said. "Something scary happened at Halcyon House today, so we're not going to go there any-more."

"Scary?"

"Yes. Remember we told you about the gun cabinet that Mr. Hutchinson has? Well, when we were there today, while I was in the kitchen talking to Carmen, Curtis opened the cabinet. I guess he'd found the key somewhere. And he and Grub went out to the stable and he was showing the gun to Grub and it went off. It didn't hit anybody, but it might have. So we're not going there anymore. Not ever again."

Mom sat down at the table. She looked shocked, horri-fied. "That's awful," she said. "And it just proves what I've always said about having guns around. . . ." She paused and then asked, "Is that what upset Grub? He is in one of his moods, isn't he? A bad one. I saw it the minute he came in. Is it because of what happened with the gun?"

Neely nodded. "Partly, I guess. The gun, and because we can't go back there anymore. Grub loved going to Hal-cyon."

"I know," Mom said. "Did you talk to him about it? About not being able to go there anymore?"

"Not exactly," Neely said. "But he knows. I think he just knows."

Of course that was the reason for Grub's mood—knowing that they couldn't return to Halcyon ever again. Neely was certain of that. So a little later she went to his room and tried to cheer him up, but nothing she said seemed to help. In fact Grub still refused to discuss it at all. Lying on his stomach on his bed, he covered his head with a pillow and told Neely he couldn't talk about it.

Neely was worried. Not that there was anything so unusual about Grub having a gloom-and-doom attack. It was just that this one seemed different, deeper and more despairing.

CHAPTER
37

THE NEXT MORNING THERE WAS NO CHANGE. GRUB WAS still sad and silent. But then, around ten o'clock, when Mom and Neely were both in the kitchen, the phone rang and Mom answered it. Neely was peeling apples at the kitchen sink and even though she could only hear Mom's part of the conversation she quickly became aware that the caller was Carmen—and that whatever she was saying was scaring Mom to death.

At first Mom said, "Why, yes. Hello, Carmen," in a normal phone-conversation tone of voice, but then she began to sound more anxious as she said, "Yes, Neely told us about the episode with the gun, and we were very concerned, of course."

After that there were many minutes in which Mom only listened and said almost nothing, except "oh no," and "how awful."

Neely stopped peeling apples and just watched while

Mom's eyes grew wide and fixed and her tanned face faded to a strange grayish color. Finally, in a shaky voice, she said, "How terrible for you and his parents. And thank you, Carmen. Thank you so much for letting us know. And about Grub . . . I just don't know. I'll talk to my husband and call you back as soon as we decide what to do."

Mom sat down at the kitchen table and stayed there for a long time with her head in her hands, and when Neely asked her what Carmen had said she would only say that she would have to talk to Dad first. Neely went on asking until Mom got angry and yelled at her. Mom called the motel then, but it turned out that Dad had gone on some errands in Monterey and couldn't be reached right away. So Neely had to wait and wait some more. And even after Dad finally got home there was more waiting because he and Mom went immediately into the study together. They stayed there for a long time and when they came out they both went into Grub's room. Even by standing very close to Grub's door Neely couldn't hear exactly what they were saying, but after a while she could hear Grub sobbing.

It wasn't until they came out of Grub's room and had gone back to Dad's study that Dad asked Neely to come in. Taking hold of her arm, he led her over to sit between him and Mom on the sofa. And then came the most maddening wait of all, sitting there with her heart thudding against her ribs, looking back and forth at their pale, tense faces. It was Mom who finally began to speak.

"It was Carmen," Mom said. "The call this morning was from Carmen."

Neely nodded. "I know," she said calmly, squeezing down the urge to yell, *I know that!* "But what did she say?"

"It was about Curtis. It seems—" Mom took a deep breath—"it seems it's happened before. Curtis shot someone before."

Neely had to try twice before the word came out, "Someone?"

"One of his cousins," Mom said. "A boy about his own age. About a year ago. They were playing with the gun and it went off accidentally. At least that was what Curtis said happened, and no one could prove differently because there were no witnesses—and the other boy was dead."

Dad broke in then. "Carmen said everyone believed Curtis's story. And Carmen believed it, too, at least until yesterday. Or at least she tried very hard to believe it. Carmen loves Curtis very much. She's cared for him since he was born and he's almost like her own child. So of course she didn't want to believe that he would deliberately shoot someone. But now she's afraid that he did, and—" Dad paused, looking at Mom.

Mom took a long, quavery breath. "And she believes that he probably meant to shoot Grub too."

There was a strange noise, a gasp that was almost a moan. For a moment Neely didn't realize that it had come from her own throat. Dad reached out and took her hand.

Mom went on then, telling more about what Carmen had said about Curtis and his cousin, and the reasons she now thought the shooting had been deliberate. And then Dad said that Carmen's call was really to ask for Grub's help.

"Carmen says that unless Grub will testify about what really happened she'll never be able to convince people that Curtis must have professional help. Carmen thinks that Curtis ought to be taken away from his parents and put in a stable environment where he could get the kind of counseling he needs if he is to have any chance of a normal life. But she needs some proof of Curtis's intentions in order to convince his uncle and the authorities."

"His uncle?" Neely asked.

"Yes," Mom said. "It seems the uncle is the legal guardian. Of Curtis and of his father as well. The uncle will have to be convinced if Curtis is to get any help." Mom sighed. "And I guess that will depend on Grub. For instance, she wants to know if Grub really did ask Curtis to show him the gun, and if he didn't, why he went out to the stable with Curtis."

Remembering Grub's reaction to her questions, Neely asked, "Did Grub tell you what happened? What did he say?"

Mom shook her head. "Nothing," she said. "Nothing at all. When we tried to talk to him he hid his head, and when we insisted he became almost hysterical."

Then Dad said, "We were wondering if you'd try, Neely. If Grub would tell anyone it would probably be you."

"I already tried," Neely said, "and he wouldn't say anything. Should I try again?" Mom and Dad said yes.

❖

When she opened the door to Grub's room he was staring out the window, but when he saw her he immediately ran back to the bed and covered his head with the pillow. Neely sat down on the side of the bed and began to talk.

"I guess Mom and Dad told you about Curtis shooting someone before," she said. "About him shooting his cousin? Carmen thinks Curtis did it on purpose because the cousin always got the best of him."

Grub lay perfectly still, except that his knuckles got whiter as his grip on the pillow tightened.

"Carmen thinks Curtis is very sick and he needs lots of help, but no one else believes her. And she won't be able to get help for him unless you are willing to tell people exactly what happened yesterday."

Grub didn't move or speak.

"She really thinks you're the only one who can help," Neely said. "The only one in the world who can help Curtis."

Grub's right hand loosened then and when Neely tugged gently at the pillow he let her take it away. Still lying facedown, Grub said, "But I didn't ever get the best of Curtis."

Neely thought a minute before she said, "Yes, you did, Grubbie. You didn't mean to, but you did."

After another long silence Grub sat up, rubbed his wet eyes and said, "He did want to. He wanted to kill me. I knew he wanted to . . . before."

"Before what?" Neely asked.

"Before yesterday. I knew that day when we went up to

the ballroom. Remember, when he told you we went up there to talk about having a band?"

Neely had to swallow twice before she was able to say, "How did you know? Did he try to push you?"

Grub shook his head. "No, but he thought about it. I knew. It was like . . . somebody told me."

"Somebody?" Neely asked quickly.

Grub's gaze drifted away and then came back. "*Something*," he said. "I said, *something* told me."

Neely was getting exasperated. "But if you knew that, Grubbie, why on earth did you want to go back there? I didn't know it. Carmen told me to watch out for you, but I thought she meant because of Monica. I thought she was afraid of a ghost. I didn't know she meant Curtis. If I had known that I wouldn't ever have gone back. If you knew he wanted to kill you why did you go back?"

"Well," Grub said. "I didn't really think he would do it." He paused and then went on. "I thought something wouldn't let him do it." He smiled faintly. "And I was right, wasn't I? Something didn't let him." The smile faded and he shook his head sadly. "I just had to go back, Neely."

Neely stared at Grub, shaking her head in disbelief. "Another thing, Grubbie," she said finally. "Why on earth did you go to the stable with him yesterday? Why did you do that?"

"He said I had to," Grub said. "He said I had to or he would go out and shoot Lion. And then when we got to the stable he was just starting to put bullets in the gun when Lion came in."

Neely sat for a long time in stunned silence. When she could finally speak again she asked Grub if he would tell the truth about what happened, to help Curtis. If he would tell so that Curtis could be taken someplace where he could be helped to become a normal person. And Grub said yes. He stared up at the ceiling for a long time, but then he said yes, he would tell. Then he lay back down and pulled the pillow over his face.

Grub stayed in his room all the rest of the day. It was obvious that he was still feeling very bad. But when Mom and Dad came back in he told them just what he'd told Neely, and when they asked him if he would tell strangers like Curtis's uncle and the police, he said he would. Even when Mom and Dad told him he didn't have to, and it was all up to him, he went on saying he would tell. But then he went back to staring out the window with sad, empty eyes.

It was late that same night when Grub came into Neely's room and shook her awake. "Listen," he was saying. "Listen, Neely."

She heard it then, too, the wailing rise and fall of a siren. She jumped out of bed and together they hurried back to the window in Grub's room in time to see two fire trucks turning up Hutchinson Road.

When the trucks disappeared they ran out into the backyard where they could see the flashing red lights moving on up the hill, past the Jensens' and on into the Halcyon Grove. Mom and Dad came out then in their bathrobes and the four of them stood huddled together near Robinson's grave and watched a fierce red glow that grew higher and brighter against the night sky. Halcyon House was on fire.

CHAPTER
38

THE BRADFORDS STAYED IN THEIR BACKYARD FOR ALMOST two hours that night, shivering in the cold foggy air and watching until the red flames died away. When the fire trucks and police cars finally stopped going up and down Hutchinson Road the family went in the house and listened to the radio for a long time before they heard the news. Although Halcyon House had indeed burned, there had been no injuries. All the occupants of the old mansion, the news report said, had safely escaped the flames.

It was almost morning by then, but when Neely finally went back to bed she still couldn't sleep. Instead, she lay awake for a long time thinking and grieving. Grieving for the beautiful old house and for all the star-crossed Hutchinsons who had looked for peace and beauty on Halcyon Hill, high above the edge of the world. She couldn't stop thinking about how tragic it was that they had come to that beautiful place looking for peace and happiness and had so often found pain and sorrow instead.

And, of course, she grieved for herself, too, and for her own tragic loss. For Neely Bradford's loss of what had been the most exciting secret, the most wonderful mystery, and the most fascinating tragedy of her entire life. She grieved, too, for the loss of Halcyon House, for the lost beauty of all the grand old rooms and beautiful furniture, and in particular for the wonderful dollhouse. She grieved especially long and hard for the dollhouse. But perhaps most of all, she mourned for the loss of the mystery of Monica.

Monica. The loss of Monica. A sudden anxiety made Neely slip out of bed and tiptoe across the hall and into Grub's room. Grub was awake too. In the dim glow from his night-light Neely could see that he was lying on his back staring up at the ceiling. "Hi," he said as she bent over his bed. "Did you want to tell me something?"

"No," she said. "I just wanted to see if you were all right."

Grub didn't smile but his eyes were wide and calm. "I'm all right," he said.

Strangely enough, it seemed to be true. And, to Neely's surprise, all the next day Grub seemed to be pretty much his usual self. A little quieter perhaps and certainly not bouncing and humming, but not at all in a full-fledged gloom-and-doom attack, either.

He went on being fairly cheerful even on Monday, which, because of the start of a new week of school, was apt to be a bad day for Grub. And even the interview, sched-uled for a few days later, didn't seem to worry him very much. Which really surprised Neely, particularly since it seemed to worry Mom and Dad a lot.

By standing outside doors and around corners, Neely had overheard enough to know that Mom and Dad had seriously considered refusing to allow Grub to testify about what had happened. Grubbie was such a sensitive kid that they were afraid it might be too hard on him. In fact it wasn't until they'd had several phone calls from Carmen, and Curtis's uncle, Harold Hutchinson the third, that they changed their minds and said yes.

On the day of the interview Curtis's uncle and Carmen and a police officer and a psychologist came to the house and had a long meeting with Mom and Dad and Grub in the living room. Neely waited outside the living room door but she could only hear an occasional word or two. She was getting pretty frustrated when Mom came out with Grub.

Grub looked quite calm. In fact he looked almost pleased with himself, as if he'd really enjoyed being the center of so much attention. For some reason Neely felt a little irritated. She was frowning at Grub when Dad came out into the hall and asked her to come in.

So then Mom took Grub off to the kitchen and Neely went in to be interviewed. In the living room Carmen, looking much more dressy than usual, was sitting in Neely's favorite overstuffed chair, Harold Hutchinson the third and the psychologist were sitting on the sofa, and Dad and the policeman were standing by the fireplace. The psychologist and the policeman were all dressed up in suits and ties, but Harold the third was wearing khaki slacks and a sweater. He looked serious but friendly, and to Neely's relief not at all like any Hutchinson she'd seen before, either in person or in a portrait.

When Dad introduced Neely they all said hello and Harold the third stood up and shook her hand. Then Neely stepped back, looked around at everybody—the way she did when she was giving a talk at school—and began. "Well, Curtis called on Saturday morning and asked if we could come up and I—" but at that point Dad interrupted.

"Neely, I think there is just a particular question that we still need to have answered. I think we need to find out if you know of any reason why Curtis might have been angry at Gregory."

"Oh," Neely said, feeling a little bit let down. After thinking for a moment she said, "Well, yes. I can think of quite a few things actually. Mrs. Hutchinson raved about Grub—Gregory, that is—all the time. Like she was always saying how cute he is, and everything. And that always seemed to make Curtis angry. And then the way Grub and Lion loved each other. That seemed to bother him a lot. Actually, he seemed to get angry whenever anyone paid too much attention to Grub." She thought of adding, "particularly when I paid too much attention to him," but she decided against it. She really didn't want to get into any of that stuff about Curtis being in love. But then Carmen more or less did it for her by telling everybody how Curtis's relationship with Neely seemed to be so important to him. Neely was a little disappointed that there weren't any other questions she needed to answer.

Later when they were all leaving, Harold Hutchinson the third thanked all the Bradfords for their help. He particularly thanked Neely and told her that her testimony and Grub's would make it possible for Curtis to get the best possible chance to turn his life around and grow up to be normal. Neely thought Harold the third seemed like a sensible person, and she felt good that Curtis had him and Carmen. He was going to need people like them.

It was only a day or two later when Reuben drove into the Bradfords' yard in his pickup truck and asked to speak to Dad. It seemed that Reuben was going away to work for Curtis's uncle in San Diego, and since there was no place for a dog where he'd be living, he wondered if Grub could have Lion. Grub was reading an encyclopedia at the kitchen table when Dad came in to tell him, and even before Dad stopped talking Grub was on his feet dancing around the room so wildly that he broke a coffee mug and tipped over the garbage pail before Neely was able to drag him outside where he could finish celebrating without destroying the whole house.

Only a couple of weeks later, on a cold, windy evening, Grub and Neely and Lion were lying on the living room floor in front of a fire in the fireplace. Grub had been scratching Lion's stomach and humming softly to himself. Neely had been trying to read, but for some reason she was finding it hard to keep her mind on the story.

Something, perhaps the leaping red flames in the fireplace, kept taking her mind back to the red glow above the hills and to the sad story of Halcyon House. She thought first about the mystery of the fire, and wondered again about how it started. According to the newspapers there had been an official inquiry and lots of possible causes were investigated. Like someone smoking in bed, for instance, or playing with matches, or just some sort of wiring problem. But apparently the official investigation hadn't been able to prove anything at all. Another Halcyon mystery.

She thought next about the mystery of Harold the first and his hopeless search for peace. And then again about poor, sad Curtis, and finally . . . about Monica. The terrible, tragic mystery of Monica that would never be solved now that Halcyon House was gone.

Something was getting on her nerves and she realized suddenly that it was all that cheerful humming.

"Grub," she said irritably. "Would you please stop that awful racket? I can't keep my mind on what I'm reading."

Grub stopped humming. He looked surprised and hurt, and when Neely glanced up a little later he was still watching her out of the corners of his eyes. Neely got up and went to the window.

Looking down the long slope to the sea, where an almost full moon was turning the ocean waves into snaky ribbons of glittering foam, she went on being angry for a moment—and then began to wonder about it. It didn't take long to figure it out. She was angry at Grub because he was so happy. Because, instead of being brokenhearted about losing Monica, as she had expected him to be, he seemed to have forgotten all about her. And so quickly. One day he'd been sad and gloomy and the next—the very next day after the fire, in fact—he'd been right back to normal. She wondered why. She really wanted to know why.

Back in front of the fire, standing now and leaning against the mantel, Neely stared down at Grub, frowning a little. And he stared back, wide-eyed, a little bit wary.

Neely took a deep breath. "Grub," she said. "What about . . . I mean . . . don't you ever think about—about Monica?"

Grub stopped scratching Lion's stomach. For a moment he returned Neely's stare and then he looked away.

"Don't you?" Neely didn't mean to, but she knew she sounded accusing.

Grub shook his head. "No," he said. "Monica's not there anymore." He paused, chewing on his lower lip. Then he smiled and said, "I think she's not lonely now. Not anymore."

Neely dropped down to her knees. "Really?" she said. Her mind was racing. Suddenly she knew exactly what Grub meant. "Do you mean that she couldn't go away while the house was there? And the nursery, and all her things? Like all those things of hers kind of held her there against her will. And now she can go to—to wherever she's supposed to be. That's what you meant, didn't you, Grub?"

Grub looked pleased—and a little bit surprised.

"I did?" he said.

Neely's sigh was long and satisfied. Satisfied because . . . well, even though she'd always been fascinated by tragic stories, she really didn't have anything against a little bit of "happily ever after" when you came to the last page.

Zilpha Keatley Snyder has written many distinguished books for children, including *The Egypt Game*, *The Headless Cupid*, and *The Witches of Worm*, all Newbery Honor Books and American Library Association Notable Books for Children. Her most recent books for Delacorte Press are *Cat Running*, *Fool's Gold*, *Song of the Gargoyle*, and *Libby on Wednesday*.

Zilpha Keatley Snyder lives in Marin County, California.